FAMILY, LOVE, & RIVALS

A Railers Novella Collection

RJ SCOTT
V.L. LOCEY

Love Lane Books

Family, Love, and Rivals

A Railers Novella Collection

All Rights Reserved

Dedication

To my family who accepts me and all my foibles and quirks. Even the plastic banana in my holster.
VL Locey

Always for my family,
RJ Scott

Christmas

A RAILERS NOVELLA

Baby MAKES THREE

RJ SCOTT &
V.L. LOCEY

Chapter One

JARED

February

I hated waking up to a Ten-sized space in bed but in the last few weeks it had become the norm. Missing the early morning snuggling was one thing, but knowing that my normally unflappable husband woke every day with his thoughts in a twist was hurting my heart. As I tugged on sweats and a T-shirt and resolved to hunt him down, I didn't know what I'd find.

Day one of waking at dawn I'd found him running hell for leather on our treadmill, day two it was weights, day three he was slamming pucks at the net in our large backyard, then day four we were back to running. It was twenty-one days since we'd gotten the letter from the Harrisburg Central Family Agency, and I had no idea what Ten could be doing today. Hockey players were a superstitious lot, but I was convinced this new daily ritual he'd formed was less about helping his game and more about escaping his worries.

I grabbed coffee and the specific protein shake Ten had on game days and went searching for him, finding him in the home gym. Only he wasn't running, or lifting weights; he was sitting on the treadmill, his elbows on his knees and his head in his hands. He was a sight for sore eyes, his dark hair soft and messy around his face, his Railers T-shirt with his number was old and worn and hugged him like a second skin, and his shorts meant that I got a good peek at his long legs and spectacular hockey thighs. But it wasn't any of that that I focused on—it was the look of misery on his face.

The Railers were on top of the division by five points, he'd played with a fire that blew away the opposition, and the team was on a high. So I was sure it wasn't hockey that was playing with his mind. Also, he'd only just had another checkup so I hoped it wasn't his brain that was causing him issues. He had headaches sometimes, moments when words didn't immediately come to him, but that was a small non-issue according to the specialist, just remnants of the trauma.

I was sure it was tomorrow that was messing with his head, but then it *was* a big day for us both. Stress and worry frustrated him, and that was why he'd reverted to routines.

"Babe?" I called from the door.

He glanced up at me. "Hey," he murmured.

"You worried about Philly?" I knew he wasn't, and also knew full well what his answer would be. At least it would raise a smile.

He huffed. "The day I worry about playing hockey is the day hell freezes over."

"Good." I deliberately didn't push him to tell what the *actual* reason was, always kept it to hockey, because one day he'd tell me the truth. I almost left him to his thoughts, but it appeared that today was the day he'd decided to share.

"Jared? It's not hockey, it's all these worries about what we're doing."

My stomach fell. "About trying for a baby?" We'd made the decision together, on Christmas Day, and had talked the issue to death until we were both completely sure we were on the same page. Ten wanted a family with me, I wanted a family with him, and at the end of it we'd hugged and agreed that the time was right.

"No, not that."

"What about then? Do you want to talk?"

"You're going to think I'm stupid," he muttered and rubbed his eyes.

"Never."

"Well, what if our surrogate hates us?" he blurted.

And there it was. Twenty-one days ago we'd had an email confirming a potential match from our choices, and twenty-one days ago Tennant Madsen-Rowe had begun to lose his shit. I instinctively knew that was the thing messing with his head, but it was up to him to process it all and let me in when he reached a point where he couldn't keep it inside anymore.

I handed him the shake, and settled next to him on the treadmill, bumping elbows. "What is there to hate?"

"Where do I start?"

I winced at the resignation in his voice. As his coach I needed his head in the game today, but as his husband and lover I wanted to make everything right for him. "You know she picked us from the list, right?"

"Yeah, but—"

"No buts, babe. We ticked all the boxes, same-sex married couple, sportsmen, annual income, family history, your injury and recovery backed up by doctor letters, my divorce, Ryker, wills, trusts, suggestions for contacts, references, there was nothing we left off, so if she chose us then she made decisions based on facts."

"She can still pull out of it all."

I put an arm over his shoulders and tugged him close. "She could, and you know what? We'll deal with that if it happens. Together."

"What if we go all the way to the end and—?"

"Stop thinking ahead. Let's take each day as it comes. Treat it like hockey and take each day on its merits, where each win and loss forms a tapestry of content to get us to the finals."

He laughed, and I knew I'd broken the fears for the moment. "Dude, did you just use the word 'tapestry' in a sentence about hockey?"

"I have mad English skills," I said with a smile and pressed a kiss to his stubbled cheek. He faced me and the kiss changed from a peck to a full blown hello and good morning.

Ten would be fine and we'd make it through the game, and then hell, we'd rock the meeting tomorrow with the potential surrogate.

Together.

. . .

Isobel Mackie was thirty-one, a beautician, married to Eddie, and with a twin brother, Adam, who was gay. Isobel had signed up with the agency when her brother had been going through the same process as us to become a dad with his husband. In a selfless exchange of love, she'd offered to become a surrogate because her brother was now the father of twin boys by using the same method. That was one of the things that had drawn her to us the most; that she knew what the process had been like for the brother she adored, and that her family supported her one hundred percent. In fact, her husband, Eddie, was with her today as her advocate, and there was so much love between them that it was like looking in a mirror at Ten and me. The four of us were ushered into a plush room to sit at a round table with the agency owners and a young woman called Michelle who was there to take notes.

We shook hands, exchanged pleasantries, all very formal when all I wanted to do was hug Isobel until she squeaked. Of course that would be after I explained to her that Ten was sure she was going to back out, and then begged her not to.

"It's so nice to finally meet you in real life." She smiled broadly.

"And you," I said when Ten stayed quiet. I knocked my shoe against his, but he was focusing on the paperwork in front of us.

"Do you have any questions for me?" Isobel asked with an open smile, and I knew Ten had a thousand, but again, silence.

"This is the time to discuss the finer points," Lloyd, the

owner of the Harrisburg Central Family Agency encouraged, but Ten seemed tense.

"Ten?" I murmured, "You want me to—?"

"No, it's okay," he said, then lifted his chin. "I'd prefer this meeting to be just the four of us in here, with Michelle as our case manager," Ten interrupted.

"For a high profile situation we usually oversee," Lloyd said.

"Actually, we'd prefer it to be Michelle," Isobel murmured.

Lloyd glanced at his wife, Jennifer, the other half of the ownership team, but Jennifer shrugged.

"Okay, if that's the way it has to be, then Michelle has this," she said, and pushed back her chair. "Michelle, make sure you detail everything."

"Yes, ma'am," Michelle murmured, and opened the pad in front of her, making a big deal of writing the date and time at the top of a fresh page.

We waited in silence until Jennifer and Lloyd had left, and as soon as the door closed behind them I could see the tension leave Ten in a rush.

"I hope that wasn't rude. I wanted it to be us so we can get to know each other better," Ten admitted.

Eddie nodded. "Totally understandable," he said. "But, then I thought maybe they're all sniffy because you're high-profile clients."

Ten dipped his head, he hated the celebrity part of what he did, and out in Harrisburg he was recognized more often than not. "I don't want them staring at me as if I don't deserve to be here, or that we won't be the best parents." He glanced at Michelle who was still in the start position waiting to write, but who returned Ten's glance with a level stare.

"Believe me, I have noted, and *fully understand* your concerns," Michelle said, and that was all we were getting. Only there was something in her expression that spoke of a deeper understanding of Ten's worries.

We knew they were the best local agency, and from the first meeting the owners had made it clear that they supported our choices. But they'd also insisted we didn't publicly post about our progress or make what we were doing into a media circus. They called it reasonable discretion, but I felt as if they were implying we were going through this process to get an accessory to our *lifestyle* and not because we wanted a family. I was probably wrong to even think that, but still, the concern had been there on my list of pros and cons.

I liked Michelle though, a quiet woman who appeared to respect what we were doing.

"Actually, can Jared and I have *you* as our specific case officer and put it in writing?" Ten asked Michelle.

Michelle appeared startled, but then stared down at the notebook. "You can request whomever you want," she admitted after a short pause.

"We request you as well," Isobel said, and Eddie added his agreement.

"Okay then," Ten said with enthusiasm, "can you write that down. Number one, Mr. and Mr. Madsen-Rowe request Michelle as the official case manager."

"And Mr. and Mrs. Mackie," Isobel added.

Michelle was flustered at first, and then she pulled on

her game face and sat back in the chair a little more relaxed.

"Let's get down to business then."

The next few hours were spent working through the surrogacy structure, the financial and emotional investment from both sides. We spoke at length about why Isobel was ready to do this, and she spoke so eloquently about her twin. Some of it was technical and dry, the fact that we would have an anonymous egg, with Ten's sperm, and that Isobel was our gestational surrogate. The rest? That was laughter, and getting to know each other, and finally ending up leaving the agency with the four of us going for lunch. We'd signed reams of paperwork and Michelle was collating and copying and sending our contracts.

Everything in writing even this early before conception was an issue. We'd already had a home assessment, criminal and records checks, and Isobel had been screened alongside us. There were extra NDA pages to sign so that Isobel didn't go out and sell our story to the media, and even though I wanted to say blindly we trusted her, we had to have that level of protection.

I had to keep my family safe.

Isobel had us sign anonymity forms, and our own type of NDA that we wouldn't out her as our surrogate unless she chose to reveal it. Michelle appeared to have every eventuality listed, and lawyers had prepared everything. It was reassuring, and overwhelming all at the same time.

We had an egg donor chosen, no name or identification, but we had enough information and we'd asked for very little in the way of qualifying data. We didn't care about some of the more specific stuff like hair color and eyes, because who knew what genetics would play a part in the baby we would end up loving? Yes, we crossed all the Ts and dotted all the Is but now we wanted to know Isobel, the person.

She was lovely, there was no other word for it, and even though we knew the dry details, I wanted to know more about her, but she beat me to it.

"At sixteen we fell pregnant," she blurted out, and Eddie squeezed her hand. "We'd been dating since eighth grade, and I knew I'd be with him forever. But me getting pregnant was the final straw for my parents. They not only had a gay son in my twin brother, but they had a daughter who was expecting a baby outside of marriage. Let's just say both myself and my brother were encouraged to leave home."

Of course we'd read all of this in her profile, but to hear her say the words and know that her parents had rid themselves of two children at the same time, was heartbreaking.

"She didn't need them," Eddie said, "both Isobel and Adam moved in with my mom and we did okay."

"We got married, and our first son, Dale, was born just after my seventeenth birthday, and our second, Austin, when I was nineteen. We worked for Eddie's mom in a salon in town and we were a family. When my twin, Adam, met his husband and wanted a baby, I offered to carry a baby for them." She glanced at her husband. "*We* offered. But it worked out better for all of us to have anonymity, and I promised myself that we would help another couple who couldn't have children. When we read your profile, we knew it had to be you."

"Thank you." Ten was choked.

"Of course, when we matched and they revealed who you were we nearly rethought it," Eddie said, and my chest tightened. "Only because I'm a New York fan."

"Someone has to be," Tennant deadpanned, and like that, the ice was broken.

I knew we were in good hands. She was very open about why she was willing to carry our baby, using the money to fund her education and to give her kids a good start in life, and I wanted to hand everything over to her there and then. Ten relaxed as lunch continued, and we were done. We hugged her goodbye, thanking her so much she was scarlet with pleasure. We headed back to the parking garage, and Ten tugged me into a dark corner, and held me as if he'd never let me go.

"We're doing this," he whispered in my ear.

I grinned and held onto him. "We're *so* doing this."

The disappointment was real when the first cycle didn't work. February was a hard month mentally and physically for us both. The Railers were fighting tooth and nail in a close division, tensions were high on ice, and the call from Michelle to explain there would need to be a second try rocked our safe little world.

"We get everything so easy." Ten grasped my hand hard after the call ended, "I just expected this to be easy as well."

"We don't get everything easy," I said, and tugged him

to sit next to me on the couch. "We work hard at everything, and this is no different."

We entered the second month with renewed hope, and the day we would find out if everything had worked was the day after a brutal game against Brady's Boston Rebels. Ten had been slammed into the boards in so many different ways that he was a mess of bruises, and he was exhausted. We'd slept late, but at least when I was woken by my cell phone dancing on the bedside table, he was curled up next to me.

I reached for the phone, connected the call as soon as I saw it was Michelle.

"It's good news. Isobel is pregnant."

And in that single instant as Ten and I hugged each other, we knew our lives were about to change in the most dramatic way.

Bring it on.

Chapter Two

TEN

May

Looking at my reflection in the hotel mirror, I sighed at the sorry shape of my playoff beard. It was a pitiful thing. It was more a sprinkling of peach fuzz on my chin and under my nose, with what could *possibly* have been called a chin strap if the stupid whiskers had been thicker and actually, you know, whiskers. I should've just shaved it off and put a stop to the endless ridicule from my older brothers. Brady and Jamie had *beards*. Big, thick, bushy, manly beards. And I had… this. I poked at my bare cheeks then grabbed the razor.

"Excuse me, but what are you doing?" Jared appeared in the doorway, his golden hair rumpled from sleep, his blue eyes hooded, his balls dangling in the wind.

"It's a disgrace. It has to go," I stated then popped the plastic cover off the razor.

He padded up behind me and slid an arm around my

waist. His bristly chin rubbed against my bare shoulder around the same time his stiff dick brushed my ass. "You can't shave your beard in the middle of a playoff round," he purred, cinching me close and slipping a hand into my briefs. I inhaled sharply as he stroked my cock. His teeth grazed my throat. A shudder ran over me as the razor lowered from my face. "You'll incur the wrath of the hockey gods. You need to focus on something other than your whiskers."

"Mm," I replied, allowing my head to roll to the side and rest on his shoulder so he could feast on my neck. "You know we don't have to do this in the morning now that Isobel is pregnant."

His fingers were magic, working me up to having a raging hard-on in mere seconds.

"Maybe I *like* jerking you off in the morning. We won't worry about finding a sterile cup." He bit down on my shoulder. I hissed then rocked into his hand, my fingers slipping back around to find his hips. I tugged him into me, moaning when his cock slid up between my ass cheeks. "How badly do you want to come, Ten? Tell me."

A groan bubbled up out of me. He was rough as he pumped me, rolling his palm over the head of my dick, smearing pre-cum over my length as he flicked his hips up and down.

"Pretty badly," I confessed, eyelids closing as I gave myself over to him. We'd been married for several years now and still his merest touch set me on fire. "*Really* badly."

"Stupid late flights," he huffed, his cock gliding

between my cheeks while he worked me faster and faster. My fingers bit into his hips. "God I love watching you get close, babe." A spark lit off at the base of my spine. I rocked back into him, gasping as my orgasm sat just out of reach. "You look incredible, so wanton, so masculine. My beautiful husband."

My balls drew up. I turned my head to beg for a kiss. Jared knew what I needed; he *always* knew. His mouth captured mine in a sloppy kiss. I jerked and covered his hand with spunk. He groaned into my mouth, his tongue knotted with mine, then blew his load all over my lower back.

"Oh shit," I panted, my cock pulsing. He gave me a few slow tugs then lifted his fingers to my face. Watching him in the mirror as he smeared my warm spunk over my lips was intense. Then he twisted my head toward him and cleaned it off with long, hungry swipes of his tongue. Then he dipped inside, licking at my teeth and tongue as if starved.

"Okay, I am not going to be worth shit at morning skate," I sighed after the kiss ended. His smile was pure ego. "Yeah, yeah, you the man."

"Keep that in mind the next time you start on about all the gray whiskers." He patted my backside then led me to the shower. It was a tight fit. Most hotel showers weren't made for two burly hockey players. I loved the gray coming into his hair and beard. Those silver hairs turned me on. Everything about Jared got me hot. It had always been that way.

When we turned off the water I stole one final kiss. As Jared reached for the towels someone pounded on the door.

"I swear if that's Adler with another stupid plunger," Jared huffed.

I snorted in amusement. Adler had been really into this whole "Plunge Pittsburgh" media campaign that he swore Layton had come up with but we all knew it was him. He'd been the first to use the hashtag. Now every store in Harrisburg was sold out of plungers. Fans tried to bring them to the games back home. It was plunger chaos. And we still had to beat Pittsburgh now, in their own dojo. We'd arrived in the Burgh tied at one game apiece in the eastern conference semifinals.

"Chill out, gramps. I'll get it. You find your Metamucil and take a big gulp. It'll help put a smile on your face."

He slapped my ass playfully as I darted out to the room, found a pair of shorts, and yanked them up over my wet ass. Grinning widely because life was fucking great, I yanked the door open to find Stan waiting. He'd just come up from the hotel swimming pool. His wet hair and the smell of chlorine was a surefire clue.

"Ah, I think to give up for knocking and suppose that you and Jared are making wild bison sex. I get ready to go back to my room and see if Erik is waking up yet. But you are not fucking like ferrets, so I come in and talk!"

The big man pushed past me, waved at a still naked Jared, who slammed the door in Stan's face, and then flopped down in a padded chair by the desk.

"Won't you come in?" I tossed out.

"I have already come in. Is your brain not working fast yet today?" His gray eyes narrowed.

"Nah, buddy, I'm fine. I was being sarcastic." I sat on

the end of our king-sized bed. "What did you need to talk about?"

"Well, I am having Mama and then all children go through attic. We have much baby things. Hundreds of tons! Clothes, cribs, little baby walker things with wheels that baby races around in." He made his fingers walk to show me how the baby walker thing worked. I chuckled. "We also have cranky baby swing thing, and clothes. Toys! Many boxes of toys! I tell Mama to pack up all the things for little newborn and send to you. When we are home you will find boxes up to ceiling in garage. You are welcome. I can see you are happy beyond making words. This I do for you as your best friend. Also, we need attic space."

"I uhm… wow!" I said, stunned at the mental image of what our garage must now look like. "Thanks!" I held up my knuckles and he rapped them soundly. "You didn't have to do that. We were more than happy to go buy new for him or her."

"Pah, for yes I did. You are my best friend on team. Stuff is good, like new, only a few bite marks where Noah chew on crib rail." He chomped his teeth. "Other than bite marks, like new for the coming little one!"

"Well, thanks. Oh, hey, are you up for a Pokémon team meeting during lunch? Rumor has it the new Pokémon Go! is about to launch."

"Ah! Yes, I am so big for going in the Pokémon!" He pushed to his feet. Jared exited the bathroom, his cheeks pink from being caught with his ass showing. "Hello. You are looking red in face. Did you take bad hot shower?"

"No, it's from shaving." Jared padded over to the dresser, his towel tightly knotted around his waist.

"But face is full of whiskers. I bring you new razor!
Sharp like Ginsu TV knife!"

And off Stan went in search of a Ginsu razor for Jared.

"How can he be so chipper so early in the morning?"
Jared asked.

"He's just one of those kind of guys. Oh, and we have
a garage filled with baby stuff. Not sure where we're going
to put all the crap Brady and Jamie and my mother are
sending. Maybe we can open a used baby goods store."

He chuckled softly. I rolled to my side to enjoy the
view as he dropped his towel and rummaged in his bag for
underwear. For a man creeping up on forty his body was
fucking stunning. Tight, firm, still thick with muscles.
Nice hockey bubble butt and meaty thighs.

My dick was perking up as I looked at him. His phone
began to buzz on the desk. Figuring it was Ryker calling
from Arizona, I flopped to my back and began thinking of
breakfast, and the game tonight. I felt that I needed to do
better for our team. It had been a few years since we'd last
clinched the Cup, and some of our players were getting
older. We had a window this season that we might not have
again for a few years. I'd only gotten one assist in the last
game and that wasn't good enough. The Railers were
depending on me to—

"Yes, no, stay there with her."

I sat up on the bed, all musing of hockey fleeing as
Jared's tone was troubled. Had something happened to
Ryker? His ex?

"Isobel is bleeding," he whispered and my whole
world sort of skewed off-center.

"Bleeding? Like…you mean womanly bleeding?"

Ugh, I was stupid. How could I possibly be a father if I couldn't even use proper medical terms for female anatomy. What if we had a daughter? Jared nodded. I shot up off the bed. "We're going home. *Now*."

"Tennant, hold on, please. We can't just fly home during a playoff round unless it's a verifiable medical emergency," Jared said then resumed talking to Eddie. I raced around the room, whipping clothes I'd dropped on the floor back into my suitcase. "Yes, please, let us know what's happening. Give her our love and best wishes. Thanks, Eddie. We'll be praying for her." He moved to me, stilling my mad packing with a hand on my arm. My gaze flew from my suitcase to my husband. "Ten, stop. There is nothing we can do right now. Eddie is with her in the ER. They're going to check her out thoroughly to see if they can find the cause."

"Is she going to lose the baby?" It was all I could think of. I'd spent so many nights lying next to Jared, my cheek on his chest, as we planned and dreamed of our child. If we lost him or her now I just...I didn't know what I would do.

"No." He sounded sure but his sad eyes betrayed him. "I hope not. Ten, there are lots of reasons women spot during early pregnancy."

"Like what?" I refused to stop packing; he could eat my shorts. I had them right in my hand.

"Well, I'm not sure but there are. When Ryker's mom was carrying Ryker she had a small scare."

"Yeah?" I stalled, the panic subsiding.

He nodded. "Let's give the doctors time to check

Isobel out. We'd only be in the way, adding to her stress, if we were there."

"I am *not stressed*!" He crossed his arms and gave me that patented Jared Madsen arched eyebrow. "Okay, yeah, I might be stressed." I flung my shorts into my open suitcase then flipped the lid shut. "What if she loses the baby?"

He sat on the bed then tugged me down beside him. "If that happens, which we will pray it doesn't, but if it does then we'll try again in a few months." He draped an arm around my shoulder then kissed my damp hair. "We need to send good vibes to her though, so let's try our best to think positive thoughts, okay?"

"Sure, yeah, of course. I'll think good thoughts."

We sat there for a few minutes, soaking up each other's strength. I did my best to send out healing vibes but fear made it hard to keep the good thoughts at the fore.

I ate something during our team breakfast. What kind of food I had no clue. It filled me up. Jared sat beside me, talking to Dieter about some ice skating forum that Trent was attending in Amsterdam. They thought they might spend the summer there if he could talk Trent into leaving his rink in Philly for that long of a time.

Morning skate was a mess. I was unable to concentrate and I gave up pretending I was fine. I made up some lame excuse about having a stomach ache from the late night run we'd made to Primanti Brothers as soon as we'd gotten to the hotel. One did not spend time in Pittsburgh and not hit up Primanti Brothers. There was a law, I think.

I showered alone, which was a blessing, as my mood

was dark and dour. I couldn't stop thinking about Isobel and the baby. We had a garage full of stuff. Hopes and dreams. I'd never felt this connected to one tiny person in my life. I'd thought my love for Jared was mind-boggling, and it was, but this was something different. Just as strong, but different. I scrubbed at my sickly beard, using my fingernails to rake out the sweat from my time on the ice.

"Tennant," I heard Jared calling over the rushing water. I closed my eyes, rinsed the soap from my face and body, and then shook like a dog. "Ten, Eddie's on the phone." I blinked the water from my eyelashes, cranked off the taps, and then grabbed a towel from the mound by the door. I studied my husband's face intently as I closed the distance. "She has a yeast infection which caused the spotting."

"Oh." I had no clue what that even was. Like, was that sort of something similar to athlete's foot for a vagina? God I was stupid. "The baby?"

"Is fine. Come here, they want us to listen to something." He led me from the massive shower room to the dressing room. My wet feet were making squeaky noises in my Crocs. "Okay, here."

He handed me his phone and I placed it to my ear. "Hello?"

"Hi, Tennant," Isobel said. She sounded okay. Not in pain or anything. "I'm sorry to have scared you. Everything is fine with the peanut. Just some spotting from the infection."

"Yeah? Are you sure?"

"Yes, the doctors are positive. They're listening to the heartbeat now during an ultrasound. Would you like to hear?"

Jared smiled and leaned in close, kissed my cheek, then rested his head next to mine. "Yeah, we'd love to hear the heartbeat!"

I tipped the phone so Jared could hear clearly. At first I couldn't really figure out what I was hearing. I was expecting that *thump-thump-thump* of an adult heartbeat. But this wasn't at all like that. It was a swishy, rapid *whoosh-whoosh-whoosh-whoosh* that made my eyes get teary. Jared coughed lightly then we both sort of fell into each other's arms in relief.

"Thank you, Isobel! Thank you so much," I gushed, hanging on to Jared for dear life.

"You're welcome. I am *so* sorry for scaring you. Jared told Eddie that you were going to fly home to be here. That's just… well, it's really sweet. We have pictures from the ultrasound. Would you like them?"

"Yes! Please, thank you again!"

Then the image from the ultrasound arrived on Jared's phone with the *ping* of an incoming message. We studied the black and white picture for a moment. I turned the phone this way and that but couldn't see a baby.

"Here, this is the baby. See this little person with tiny limb buds and a super-strong heart. He gets that from you," Jared teased, but the worry of the heart condition was one of the reasons we'd used my baby batter.

"Oh wow, it's like the most beautiful little person with limb buds that I've ever seen. Do you see a dick?"

He laughed out loud as I squinted and brought the phone close to my nose.

"It's too soon to tell, but I agree, it's a beautiful little person."

"Ah man, that's our kid!" I kissed him on the mouth and ran out of the dressing room in only my Crocs and a towel. I had to show the rest of the team our baby. I bumped into a female reporter, blushed hotly, and then ran back into the dressing room for clothes and my husband. Together we waited, hand in hand, for the Railers to leave the ice and fawn over our baby. *Our. Baby.*

Chapter Three

JARED

June

The desolation was real. Game seven and we'd been outplayed by a determined Carolina team who now advanced to the final. The series had been so close, and I couldn't have hoped for a better team out there, but the silence in the locker rooms was heavy. There had been shining moments in my journey as coach when I'd said exactly the right thing to motivate, and sometimes it meant I had to lie. Coach could tell the men that we had a chance against a team on a hot streak, or that injuries didn't matter, or that we were destined for great things. I could stand there and give a rousing defensive player speech about chance and fate, but as I glanced at Ten, at the way he was hunched in on himself, I knew no one could face the men in this room and not tell the truth.

"Well, shit," Coach Benning said.

Adler slipped off the bench and sprawled on the floor, exhausted, gripping Stan's leg to hold himself steady, and

Erik was red-eyed. That was just the guys close to me, but it was Ten I focused on as he glanced up at me with exhaustion lining his face. My husband had played his heart out on that ice, the same as everyone, but we had to accept that this year wasn't our year.

"You did nothing wrong," Coach began.

"I let two goals to net," Stan said.

"I fucked up in that last check," Erik sighed.

"I'm too slow," Adler moaned.

"It was chaos in the third," Arvy added.

Only it was Ten who summed up how they probably all felt. "I wasn't good enough."

Oh fuck. That last bit broke my heart, and I had no idea what to do to make it better. We knew the taste of success, we'd lifted the cup, we knew we could win, but we had to face one very important thing, that tonight we tasted loss and it was bitter, but it wasn't the first time, and it wouldn't be the last. Teams didn't win every freaking year, they were lucky if they got two in a row, but that was hockey.

Coach widened his stance. "They were the better team, and they got the luck tonight."

It was very simple really, one lucky bounce, a defender who got too close to Stan, and that second puck had hung suspended in the air with a life of its own, before slipping through the tiniest space. With only twelve-seconds on the clock, even with a time out, I knew at that moment we'd lost. We challenged but it was eventually called a good goal, and even pulling Stan there was no way we'd get a second try to score in those remaining seconds. The heart never left the team, they tried for every second, Ten on a rush, Erik right by him, but it wasn't enough.

I was just as destroyed, but for now I needed to be strong for them all, and I wished I had the words.

"Next year, boys," Connor stated simply, the reason he was captain on display. He stood, and paced around the room, still on skates, sweat dripping from him, his hair flat to his head, tapping the shin of each player. He had mentions for all of them, things they'd done in the game, and when he got to Ten he paused the longest, waiting for Ten to look up at him. When he did, Connor went to an awkward crouch. "You are good enough, Tennant Madsen-Rowe. We all are. We're the best freaking expansion team they've ever seen, and I tell you something for nothing, next year it will be us hoisting the cup. You hear me?"

I waited for Ten to argue, to lose himself in self-flagellation, but instead he gave Connor a half smile. "You know that for sure, Cap?"

Connor nodded, and then stood awkwardly, before appearing next to me. "We rocked that ice, we just didn't have the luck." He began a slow clap, and at first everyone stared at him as if he were losing his head, but he didn't stop until each of the rest of the team began to join in. Then the clapping became determined and each man rose to his skates, and the weight of loss shifted a little. It wouldn't disappear for a long time, for some of the guys on the team, including Connor, it might well have been the last chance before retirement, but every man in this room had fought for a championship ring and fought hard, and we needed to remember that.

The media interviews were rough. Connor didn't

demand anyone accompany him, as captain he would be expected out there, but Ten followed him automatically, along with Stan. Questions flew about the makeup of the team, about the coaching choices, about that final goal, but Connor handled it all with quiet, responsible answers.

"Do you think your bigger cap hits are effective players?" one guy asked from the back, and I held my breath. He was talking about Connor, Ten, Stan. How Connor deflected this was crucial and I held my breath.

"We're sitting here after taking it to game seven in the championship finals, which we lost more to a twist of luck than bad work, and you ask us that question? Next?"

Then it was our turn, but they didn't want to talk to the assistant coaches, they wanted to talk to Coach Benning. Blame him. Find fault in him and his team, and I hated that.

"Jared, a question for you? Your contract is due for renewal at the end of this season," someone called from the back of the room. "Jared, rumors are that Vancouver is looking for a new defensive coach and have put feelers out to you. How do you see that playing out?"

That was news to me, and probably complete speculation on the part of whoever was asking, but the words knifed into me. Who knew where I would go? Ten was secure here, with a no-trade clause stipulating that he'd have to agree to a move before they could do that to him. But I didn't have a contract like that. Management could turn around and tell me that I was no longer needed, or that I wasn't the best fit for the team, even if they'd given no indication that I was going to be let go. A win here would have reinforced my methods for the defense as being good, but the loss was just as much a kick to my gut as to the players.

"I don't see that playing out at all," I lied.

Disappointment hung in the air, the room thick with it, the locker room was quiet, and even Adler was quiet, and that was a miracle. But, at least we were talking about the good bits, and I was sure we'd shake it off and refocus on next year. I hadn't managed to hug Ten, or even talk to him directly yet, but when the door to my office opened and he slipped in, I pulled him close and held him for a long time.

"Well, shit," he repeated my words, then slumped against my table, tugging me with him until I slotted between his legs. We stayed that way, hugging, and everything unspoken filled the room.

"Next year, Ten. Next year."

"Next year. For sure."

Breakdown day had been tough, collecting everything together to bring home, and commiserating in detail about what had gone wrong. It didn't matter that Carolina had just lost two games in a row in the next round against a dominant Tampa Bay, because we'd collectively gotten to that point where things had begun to make sense. The Railers had played their hearts out, and they deserved to go deeper, but we'd take the summer and then come back strong and determined. The way the team rallied around me was heartwarming, and not one person mentioned the looming coach contract negotiations.

Not even Ten talked about it, but the thought of what might happen was there between us, and it was horrible.

The lethargy and unanswered questions lasted a full week when the question in the presser weighed on my mind. Only the daily reports from Isobel were enough to shift the quiet despair inside me about what the hell we'd do if I was heading to Vancouver. But it was Isobel and our child that was front and center in my thoughts. What was the point of having a child when I would be separated from them for months at a time? That wasn't being a dad, and I'd already lived through that with Ryker. The regrets about some of the enforced absences I'd had from him were acid in my gut. By the time I was due to meet with management, I'd convinced myself that if they were thinking of removing me from the team, I would tell them to go fuck themselves, and enjoy the rest of my life being a dad.

Who needs to be an assistant coach of a topflight NHL team?

Me, I thought miserably as I sat outside the conference room with Coach and one of the other assistant coaches, Pike, along with a miserable-looking Gagnon. This was going to be hard, dissecting the year, talking players, and planning for the next year.

If I still have a job.

"You can all come in now," the PA said from the door, his smile innocent enough.

I shook his hand and entered the lion's den. Coaches at my level didn't always have agents—I didn't have one —but I wished I had someone here to hold my damn hand.

"Morning," I said to all of them, taking inventory. The management consisted of five people, including the lawyer, and Owen Hargreaves, part-owner and GM of the team, stood and extended his hand to Coach.

"Next year," he muttered as we shook hands, and then he bro-hugged us all which was kind of casual if I was going to be sacked.

"Yes, sir."

"I want to close one thing down before we start, Jared, we want you for another three-year fixed contract, details to be discussed, are we good with that?"

Relief flooded me, another three years, with a team I loved, stable in Harrisburg, with Ten and our new baby? I wouldn't have cared if they'd offered me fifty dollars and a lunch voucher. "Yes." I didn't have any other words.

"Good, good, take a seat, we have to talk about our defense."

By the time I left the room I had a shiny new three-year contract, decisions had been made that left our core largely intact, and no indication that the management team didn't have faith in Coach or the team. I called Ten as soon as I was at the car, but when I'd left the house this morning he'd been in the garage with the piles of boxes and it seemed he was still there as the call went to voicemail. How I kept to the speed limit when I drove home, I don't know. I'd already been delayed after signing autographs at the arena gate and taking everyone's comments about how wonderful the Railers were to heart, but all I wanted to do was tell Ten.

He was waiting for me outside the garage, pacing, grinning, waving at me to stop. Had he heard? Had the Railers announced my contract had been renewed? Wow, things moved fast. He leapt on me as soon as I climbed out of the car, but it wasn't joy at my contract, it was something very different.

"The baby moved!" He danced with me around the car. "Our baby moved!"

His joy was infectious and I danced with him, ending up with a dip right there in front of a hundred boxes full of baby clothes. It was only after we'd kissed and hugged and danced some more with sheer glee did he pause to ask me about the meeting.

"They renewed my contract," was all I could tell him, the rest, moves of players, the future, that was something I had to keep close to my chest for now.

"Of course they did," Ten said with fierce loyalty, then kissed me hard. "Next year, Mr. Coach, we're getting our baby christened in the Stanley Cup."

"We are?"

Ten dragged me to the nearest box, pulled out a tiny brown and red onesie with a bird on it. "And guess who's in the house?"

It took me a second to realize that Ten was holding a Raptors-branded jersey, which could only mean one thing.

"Ryker's here!" I announced, and let Ten drag me into the house. This day was getting better and better.

We found Ryker in the kitchen cooking up a pan of bacon and making pancakes, Jacob sitting on the counter swinging his legs, and my heart expanded.

"Dad!" Ryker said and threw himself at me for a hug. The Raptors hadn't made it any further in the cup run than we did, but the fact that the bottom-of-the-league team had done so well was partly due to *my son*. I couldn't have been prouder.

"Ryker!" I motioned at Jacob as well, who slid off the counter and joined the hug, Tennant completing the circle.

"The baby moved!" Ten announced in the hug, which meant more hugs and congratulations. I hadn't even had time to process the fact that our son or daughter was becoming more than a blur on a scan, but I wasn't sure my heart could handle any more happiness.

News flew between us, Ryker's mom was well, his sisters good, his stepdad happy, his grandfather still an asshole. The wedding planning was going as well as it could do, and yes he was pissed that the Raptors hadn't made it any further in the cup run. Hockey connected us and it never failed to fill me with pride that Ryker was a star in his own right. It was only when the food was done and we were slumped around the table that it occurred to me I'd never mentioned the contract.

"I have some news," I said, when Ryker took a breath from telling us about Tate and Vlad and how much he loved Tate, and discussing with Ten about how Tate was an amazing skater and a good guy. "My contract with the Railers was renewed for three years."

Ryker grinned. "Of course it was, Dad." He didn't sound as if he doubted it for one minute.

We ended up by the pool, sprawled on recliners in the warm summer sun, and Jacob was talking Arizona with Ten who kept smiling at me as if he couldn't contain his excitement.

"I thought I'd messed up," I murmured to Ryker, who must have sensed worry in my voice, because he rolled up on his chair and gave me his full attention.

"It's okay, Dad. Some teams make it, some don't," Ryker said, and kept his voice low the same as me.

"Can we walk?" I asked, because some of what I had to say was just for my son. He was up on his feet in an instant, and we set off on a ramble around the large yard stopping by the trees and standing in the shade. We didn't talk as we walked, and by the time we stopped my stomach was in knots.

"What's wrong, Dad? Are you okay? Is it your heart?"

Oh shit, I'd worried Ryker without realizing it. "No, jeez, no, I'm fine. I wanted to talk to you about the baby."

"Oh god, is there something wrong?"

I pressed a hand to his chest. "Stop freaking out," I said and then sighed. "It's nothing awful, just they asked me in the post-game presser whether I knew that Vancouver wanted me."

"I saw that, but, Dad, Vancouver would be lucky to have you. Apart from Coach Carmichael you're the best one out there."

He was teasing me, and I fake-shoved him. "You know I'm better than any coach at the Craptors," I groused.

"Whatever, old man." Ryker winked.

We shoved each other again, and it went well until I got him in a hold and gave him a noogie. I knew damn well he could take me, but he'd let me have the dad thing I needed, and I loved him for it. I let him go, then leaned against the nearest tree watching him clamber up on the fence and perch there. He was so happy, with his hockey, with Jacob, and the fact that my boy was so at ease with himself, so confident and such a good friend to others was a testament to his mom. We might not have made our marriage work but Casey was a good mom.

"I wanted to apologize for not being around much when you were small."

"Haven't we already had this conversation," Ryker deadpanned, "and didn't we decide that I was fully cool with it, and that not only am I the best son ever, but you were an okay dad?"

"You said I was better than okay."

Ryker snorted a laugh. "See, you do remember."

I cleared my throat. "When that question hit me, I considered not being here for our new baby, and it hurt," I pressed a hand to my chest and Ryker frowned momentarily. "It brought back all these memories of the things I missed with the one person I should have always been there for."

"Do you remember my fifth birthday?" Ryker said after a short pause.

I wished I did remember all the details, but I would have only been in my early twenties, and I was still riding the high of being a professional hockey player. I wasn't at home much, Casey and I were not happy, and everything was a mess.

"No," I decided to be honest.

"We came to the rink, and I went out on the ice with the team, Mundy picked me up and carried me around on his shoulders, and we went so fast I thought we were flying." Sven Amundsen, aka Mundy, was a six-foot-six defender and loved it when the kids were at the rink. "You know how many kids wanted to fly with Mundy? Then when I was six, you took me to Toronto for a game, and we went to the Hockey Hall of Fame, do you remember that?"

"That was your birthday?"

"You were always calling me, sending me stuff, I spent time with you in the holidays, I was happy, and so lucky, so can we not do this again?"

"Just as long as you know, that this baby, whether it's a little boy or a girl, I will never love them any more than I love you."

Ryker jumped from the fence then and hugged me with purpose.

"I can't wait to have another brother or sister," he said, and we held each other for a while. "Hey, did you see the tiny jersey I brought for the baby?"

I set him away from me and faked a grimace. "No baby of mine will wear a Raptors jersey."

And Ryker, with a grin so wide it must have hurt, thumbed his chest. "Well, your first baby kinda already does."

We walked back, pushing and shoving, to find Jacob floating lazily in the pool.

"Ten said to tell you he's gone inside," he called up, wincing as Ryker let out a whoop and cannonballed into the pool.

Ten being inside meant kisses, and hugs, and all kinds of interesting things.

The best kind of day.

Chapter Four

TEN

July

My stomach felt as if I'd swallowed live eels. Or slugs. Maybe someone had hexed me. Or maybe it was the fact that Jared and I were sharing a small yellow exam room with Eddie and an ultrasound technician while Isobel was stretched out on a table with her belly bared.

"Are you sure you're down with us seeing your wife's stomach?" I whispered to Eddie while the sonographer coated Isobel's softly rounded belly with lube.

"If you're in the delivery room with her you'll probably see more than her belly," he replied then gave me a brotherly hug when my face went blank.

My gaze flew to Isobel who giggled at my discomfort. It was funny how close the four of us had become in such a short amount of time. She was like the sister I'd never had but always wanted. Most days when we were kids I would've run a two-fer sale on Brady and Jamie for one sweet, loving, giggly sister. I doubted a sister would make me eat bugs, or put itching powder in my jockstrap, or duct tape my Pikachu stuffed snuggle buddy into a toy Army jeep and then push it into traffic just to see what happened. Poor Pikachu. He wore tires tracks on his face for years…

"I'm uhm…yeah, sure. Lady parts." I slid closer to Jared who was fighting back a smile. "We're going to have to talk about lady parts." I'd never seen a woman's nether regions up close and personal, being gay and all, I'd not been interested. Now, Jared on the other hand…

He patted my head. "We'll have *the talk* when we get home."

I rolled my eyes at the sniggers filling the sunny room. There were duckies on the wall and a graph of what a baby looked like in utero. That poster didn't hold a candle to seeing the baby in person. Well, not really in person but as in person as we could get for now.

The sonographer described what she was seeing as she moved the wand around on Isobel's stomach. We got to check out the heart, kidneys, brain, and spine. We counted fingers and toes. The heartbeat was strong, and the baby kicked and moved around endlessly, finally settling down at the end of the exam.

"Ah okay, maybe we can take a peek at the genitals, if you all want to know?" the technician asked, her blue eyes questioning. We all looked at each other but no one said a thing.

"Okay so, yeah, I *definitely* want to know," I piped up. "But if you want to wait, Jared, we can wait."

"Nope, I'm fine with knowing." He took my hand.

"Okay then, let's see what this baby is," Isobel

announced as Eddie lingered at her side, his fingers meshed with hers.

"Alrighty, let's see what we can see," the pleasant blonde with the magic wand replied. It took a minute or two, something about making sure she had a midline sagittal view, whatever that meant. "Okay, thank goodness this baby decided to stop disco dancing or we would have never gotten this incredible view of her caudal notch."

"So it's a…girl? You used 'her,'" I asked, simply because I had no clue what the notch thing was she was talking about. The sonographer nodded and smiled.

"It's a girl," she confirmed.

I turned to look at Jared. He was grinning ear-to-ear. "We're having a baby girl," I whispered then hugged him as hard as I could. Eddie leaned down to kiss Isobel on the cheek. "Oh my God, it's a girl. We so have to tell the family when they get here tomorrow for the Fourth of July cookout. Oh! Hey, you two should come." I turned to Isobel and Eddie as the technician took a few more pictures and checked fluid levels or something.

"We don't want to intrude," Isobel replied.

"Seriously, it is not an intrusion at all. You're part of the family now. An honorary Rowe. My parents are dying to meet you, and so are my brothers and their wives. There will be like six kids… I think there's six now. So your boys will have kids to play with. Come over, please. This way you can rest and let someone else cook and clean up," I said with a wink.

"Okay, you sold me with the no cooking and cleaning up." Isobel laughed.

"Sounds good to me. I'd love to meet Jamie and Brady,

I think I have a puck from the last Rebels/Railers game," Eddie gushed.

"Bring it, Brady'll sign it," I said then leaned into Jared, my arm around his waist as we watched our daughter sleeping safe and sound. "We're going to have a daughter," I whispered once more to Jared.

He pressed his lips to my cheek and held me tightly to his side.

The great name debate would now begin. Good thing we had four more months. We'd need it for sure.

The following day the Rowe family blew into town. My parents arrived first because Dad always had to be early, no matter what. Going to the movies? Get there forty-five minutes early in case they sell out and/or so he could get a certain seat. Drove Mom nuts. So, they showed up on an early flight and Jared and I picked them up at the airport. Then, around noon, Jamie and his Lisa arrived with their two kids, and a few hours later Brady and his Lisa, Lisa number one, pulled up with their four kids and an aging lab named Bourque.

Our house was packed. I loved it but, man alive, six kids made a lot of noise. There were so many backpacks, sleeping bags, and sneakers tossed around it looked like a Marine obstacle course.

Dinner was pizza and soda because tomorrow was the Fourth and all the cooking would happen then. The kids were in the living room feeding Bourque pizza crusts and the adults were in the kitchen, enjoying the pizza and a bottle of wine.

"I'm so happy that your surrogate is coming tomorrow," Mom said then plucked a slice of pepperoni off my father's plate and gobbled it down.

"That'll give you heartburn," Dad warned. She waved him off.

"Yeah, me too. They seemed really up for it when we had the ultrasound yesterday. They have a couple of boys and—"

"You had your five-month sonogram?" both Lisas asked in tandem. I nodded warily. Jared poured Brady a little more wine but sat like a golem beside me. "Did you find out the sex?" It was uncanny how in sync they were at times.

My mother's eyes flared. She sat up and waited.

"Yeah we did but we don't want to—" I was steamrolled by my excitable in-laws and mother.

"You should have told us. You can do the gender reveal at the cookout!" Mom said.

Both Lisas nodded. I threw a pleading look at Brady who tossed up his hand—only one as the other was in a sling due to another operation on his shoulder—and stared at his pizza. Jamie suddenly found his napkin fascinating, and Dad was talking to Jared about a dinosaur show he enjoyed. Cowards, the whole lot of them.

The talk raced onward at full speed. Colored cakes and pink or blue balloons were being discussed when I slid into the conversation.

"Okay, can we just take a breath?" I asked then gave the women my most endearing smile. "Cool, thanks. So, the thing is, Jared and I don't really believe in gender-reveal parties."

"But we had one for all of our kids," Lisa and Lisa replied.

"There wasn't such a thing when I had you boys," Mom added while watching me close.

"Yeah, I know, and while lots of people have them, and that's cool if you want to, being active in the LGBTQ community has taught us that gender and genitals are two different things." I got confused looks. "See, it's possible that this baby may be not identify with its birth sex. It's just… there's so much gender stereotyping and possible future disappointment for the kid. Imagine you watch a video of your parents celebrating the fact that you're a girl when you're not a girl deep inside? Imagine how much that would hurt. So please, Jared and I really appreciate your enthusiasm but we don't want our daughter to be born with any labels. The world will slap enough of them on her without her family doing so before she's even born."

The room was quiet for the longest time. Then Brady spoke up. "That's cool, Ten. So, it's a girl and she's healthy, eh?"

I nodded. We got lots of congratulatory hugs and any further discussion of pink or blue fireworks withered away. Changing the way people think was a marathon not a sprint, as they said at the end of our hockey diversity meetings. On or off the ice, progress was made in increments.

Our backyard was so patriotic it would have made Captain America wince. Since I'd kindly blown the gender-reveal party idea to bits, the Lisas had fallen back on what we had in the house—full-blown red, white, and blue everything. Umbrellas, streamers, banners, sparklers, tablecloths, plates, cups, plastic cutlery, and napkins. Even good old Bourque had a star-spangled bandana tied around his neck. Burgers were piled on the grill, smoke billowing as fat dripped into the flames. Beans, deviled eggs, and macaroni salad took center stage on the picnic table as we set platter after platter of other cookout goodies around the Rowe favorites. Dad and Jamie supervised the charring of the meat and Brady tried to keep the kids from devolving into a manic wild pack of soap bubble ruffians. The eldest twin girls had already had a fight that had ended in tears, and Jamie's youngest had been stung by a bee. Bedlam reigned. And right into the Rowe chaos appeared Isobel, Eddie, and their sons.

Jared had met them at the door, it seemed, and escorted them through to the backyard.

"Everyone!" Jared shouted over the shrieks of children and CCR blaring out of my father's phone resting on the table beside the watermelon fruit bowl. "This is Isobel and Eddie."

I waved from my spot in the shade with the dog. Mom swooped down on Isobel and led her to the glider where they sat side by side falling into some deep gossip. Brady pulled up a chair beside me. He winced as he tried to get his big body comfortably wedged into a folding lawn chair.

"Shoulder hurt?" I asked and rubbed Bourque's belly.

"Always, both of them. Don't get old, brat." I bobbed my head as if I had any control over aging. Shit, I was closing in on thirty. "They're talking about you when you were a baby."

"Yeah, I know," I said with a sigh. "Talking about how I was the best and most adorable of the Rowe boys. Oh, and the smartest and most athletically talented."

Jamie walked over and dropped an ice cube down the back of my rainbow frog tank top. After I did a wild dance and flung the cube back at Jamie, Jared arrived with Eddie in tow. Brady was happy to sign his puck, and we gathered at the sunny end of the table, letting Isobel, Mom, the Lisas, and the pack of sweaty, grimy kids, have the shade. There we sat for hours eating, laughing, more eating, telling stories about our pasts, and more eating. Then the desserts were brought out.

By the time we were rounding up children to head to Riverfront Park for the fireworks show, I was so full I was waddling. Mom pulled me aside just outside the front door as the rest of the mob got kids buckled into seats.

"Tennant, Isobel is just lovely. And her husband is a delightful man. Their children are beautiful and so charming. You chose wisely, honey." She rose to her tiptoes, kissed my cheek, and then scampered off to ride in the back of Brady's rental minivan.

"Everything okay?" Jared asked as he closed and locked the front door.

"We got the Mom seal of approval for our surrogate choice."

His eyebrows flew up his forehead as he turned to face me. "That was fast. It took her ages to warm up to me."

"Well, you *did* lure me into a treehouse and had your way with me," I said and got an eyeroll.

"If I remember correctly, and I do because I'm not as addlepated as you like to say I am, it was *you* who led *me* into the treehouse in your parents' backyard."

I chuckled. "That's true, I confess. And for what it's worth, Mom and Dad loved you way before we started dating. You're really a loveable sort."

I stepped close and planted my lips to his on our shadowy front step. Some asshole turned on their headlights, flooding the stoop, then shouted at us in a thick Boston accent. Brady's shout sounding like this in my ears.

"Ah, fah Gad's sake get a room why don't cha?" My face screwed up. "Get in the cah. The pahk is probably wicked full already!"

"If he wasn't in a sling I'd pop him in the face," I muttered under my breath while Jared chortled. Our little girl was coming into one great family. Not that I'd ever tell my brothers they were awesome…but they were. Even Brady. Most of the time. Just not right then.

Chapter Five

JARED

September

"It's like the first day of school," Gagnon murmured at my side.

Minus the small kids and the Day-Glo backpacks, he was right. Starting back at training camp had the same excitement and expectation as that first day of school, full of hope that this year was going to be our year. It was vital we recalled that we didn't go all the way last year, but from today we're all being offered a chance to make good. Hell, this season could be *our* win, and no one could take that confidence away from any of the team. It wasn't our first day here, we'd already gone through rookies, and tryouts, and offered contracts to three new guys. Two of which went to the Colts, and the third, Jack Cookson, a scrappy twenty-year-old from Buffalo was a brand new D-man for me to hone. I wasn't sure where Jack would fit into my D-pairs, but he played nicely with Arvy in the tryouts, and I was focusing on the fact that we'd lost

Travis MacAllister over the summer when he'd announced his retirement. There was a hole to fill and Jack might have been the missing piece we needed.

We were first to the ice, waiting on the team, and I was as nervous as I was confident that we were going to come out strong this year. Most of that was Ten's enthusiasm rubbing off on me, and his highs were in direct proportion to how much good news we received from Isobel. We were getting daily updates and the latest, which arrived at three a.m. and caused Ten to fall out of bed, was that our daughter wanted Cherry Garcia, pickles, and ham, not individually. After picking himself up off the floor he read the text out loud, then climbed all over me, hugging and kissing, and whooping. Somehow we got back to sleep, but he was still on a high when we arrived at the training facility, and it was infectious to everyone around him.

"Coach," Jack arrived, his grin wide, his eyes bright with excitement.

He reminded me of myself. My first morning with Buffalo, waiting to be told where to go and what to do, was a shining moment in my memory, and the culmination of everything I'd fought so hard to achieve.

"Let's see it then," I nodded to the ice, and he glanced behind himself, uncertain.

"On my own?" He frowned and for a second or two I thought he'd call me out on making him skate out there without the team, but this was my chance to see his warm-up and I wasn't losing that.

Also, a rookie out on the ice without the team? Classic first day.

He paused with his left skate on the ice, and glanced

into the rafters where our winning banners hung. We didn't have any retired numbers yet, that would be for our core skaters when they finally hung up their skates, and one day Ten's number might be up there alongside Stan's, maybe even Adler's if he stopped being an idiot. Was Jack thinking that his name could be up there? Was he looking at our cup wins and thinking he could be part of another cup run?

"Sometimes I wish I could have my first day back on the ice again," I admitted, as Jack pushed off and circled the ice, his form relaxed, his skating strong. He wasn't the biggest of guys, but as a defenseman what he did have was a canny understanding of the game and the ability to hassle the other team. He didn't rely on brute force, he was all flashy skating and speed, and when he jumped smoothly to skating in reverse I saw something in him.

"I remember my first day, I was so freaking nervous."

I thumbed at Speedy-Jack. "He doesn't look nervous."

Jack executed a near-perfect lateral move in front of us, something that was the key to playing the rush and steering the opponent in the desired direction. A bit more force, a little less speed, some filling out and I could polish him into a great D-Man. I was excited to get started.

"Morning," Coach Benning arrived, followed quickly by Coach Pike. We were the core coaches for this team, and the expectation for results was heavy on our shoulders. "Kid looks good." He nodded at the ice as Jack flew by and rounded the net, switching to backwards, then icing to a stop. He was staring at the net, and I thought I saw his lips move. For all I know he could be praying to the hockey gods, or sending good thoughts out into the universe, but he seemed serene. A new generation of Railers.

"He has a lot of potential," I said.

"Not sure how long we'll get to keep him," Coach muttered, but I didn't have time to ask for specifics, because the team came out of the tunnel, half in white jerseys, half in black. It would be just my luck to find a rough diamond for me to lose him in a trade to another team.

Ten tapped my calf as he passed, the only public acknowledgment of what we were together, and then every single player was on the ice, a whirling chaotic mess of bodies shouting and teasing and knocking pucks in the net before Stan and Bryan got to their respective ends. Bryan laughed, Stan cursed at everyone in strident Russian, and then there was a loose game of nothing much, some passing, a warming up, and I noticed that Jack and Arvy had instinctively paired up. Not just that, but against Ten there was a spark there, he was making Ten work, and I loved how this dynamic was coming together.

When we split into our core teams, I had eight men ranged around me, and with a crack of my neck I began to pair them up, splitting Arvy and Jack and deciding that today we'd look at the distance between defender and the attacker.

"Heads-up, guys, today we're focusing on gap."

By the end of that first practice Jack Cookson had his official Adler-endorsed nickname, Cookie the Rookie. Poor kid, because it would stay with him for the rest of his career.

Although by the way he was smiling it didn't seem as if he cared.

When we got home Ten was on such a high that I shut myself in my office. Not that I didn't love it when Ten was like a kid at Christmas, but I needed to get my thoughts in order, and being a coach wasn't something I could leave at the door. After practice, Coach Benning had pulled me into the office and shut the door; never a good sign.

Rumors only, he'd begun, but I knew better than to ignore any kind of rumor. Then he began to explain a convoluted mess that involved us using Jack as a bargaining chip in a trade with the Boston Rebels of all people. I wanted to call Brady, and ask him if the rumors were true. Were they rebuilding the defense, and why? I would be asking him as a friend, and also as a brother-in-law. He'd been in a bad way in July, but I'd put it down to post-op blues, but maybe, if he was thinking of retiring, the Rebels would be losing their captain, and one of the best D-Men in the NHL. Ten hadn't said anything, but that was the thing with the brothers, the three of them pushed the limits, but when it came to team secrets they were locked vaults.

I sent a quick text to Brady, just wishing him good luck for the season, and then I made some notes on what I'd seen today, filing the paperwork in neat order, and finally I was done.

I padded through the kitchen, wondering where Ten was, searching downstairs, and then realizing that the one place I needed to check was the nursery. We'd decided the room at the back of the house, with the attached bath, and right next to ours, was the perfect room for our daughter, and I recall he'd muttered something about Cherry Garcia and scarlet paint when he'd stepped out of the shower today.

Leaving Ten alone in the room with his vivid imagination and an array of paint sample jars could only mean trouble, but I didn't find him painting yet more squares on the wall, I found him sitting on the deep window seat, legs crossed, staring out at the yard.

"Hey," I perched next to him.

He shuffled back to give me room. "I think I've chosen my color, or at least narrowed it down to two."

We'd agreed to choose a color each for the cozy room, and then we'd decide which we preferred, and call in an independent arbitrator if we couldn't decide. Someone who wasn't Stan or Adler. I'd already chosen mine—the original pale lemon that I thought would look cool with cream on a couple of the walls. Ryker had sent me photos of the room he'd decorated for Colorado and it was a riot of rainbow colors, including Colorado's number in dots of paint, and it suited Colorado, but I wanted this room to be an oasis of peace. I tended toward muted colors that we could then hang bright posters on, but I had no idea what Ten thought, and that wasn't the only thing we hadn't shared with each other.

The other deal was to think of one or two names and then discuss them between us. The deadline was the end of October, two weeks before our daughter was due, and that was still a way off.

"And I have a name," he added softly. "Just one, although I don't want to jinx things."

Damn hockey superstitions. "It won't jinx anything to talk about names, but we're not calling our daughter Gretsky-lina."

He smiled at me. "Damn, I was hoping you'd go for that."

"Nope, not going there, unless the middle name is Lemieux-sally," I teased and waited for him to laugh, but he appeared deadly serious.

"Charlotte," he murmured. "Charlie, Lottie, even the full name, I like that and it won't leave my head. Maybe if you think it works we could have it as a middle name?"

I laced my fingers with his. "Charlotte is perfect."

"For real?"

I'd been searching for a name that could be shortened, something that sounded right, and as soon as he'd said Charlotte my chest was tight.

"Charlotte Madsen-Rowe," I said. "How about Elizabeth for a middle name?" That had been the only name I'd held close and it was the first name of my great-grandmother. "Or Isobel?"

"Charlotte Elizabeth Isobel Madsen-Rowe," Ten said, and lifted my hand to press a kiss on my palm. "I love that."

"It's a beautiful name."

"And for the color I like the lemon we chose first, which one do you like?"

I kissed him hard, and he let out a muffled *oomph*, before cradling my face and kissing me back.

"What was that for?" he asked after our heated make-out session slowed to soft nibbles and smiles.

"Lemon was my choice as well."

He smiled broadly, his green eyes sparkling with humor. "We rock this parent thing."

"We rock it so hard."

Unspoken was the fear we both had, the usual stuff a new parent faces, such as whether we would be good parents together, or what kind of world we were bringing our baby into. Then there were the other more immediate fears, Isobel's health, our baby being born safe and well. But, for now, all we could worry about was the color of the room.

"We should go and buy paint," Ten announced and stood quickly as if he hadn't had a full day on the ice. I moved slower, muscles aching in places but with just as much enthusiasm.

"Let's go."

Sherwin-Williams was quiet, but that didn't mean the Railers' phenom that was Tennant Madsen-Rowe didn't get attention the moment he stepped inside. He'd worn a cap pulled down, neither of us were wearing Railers' gear, but this was *the* face of the Railers, and it started as soon as the greeter, a young girl with braces whose badge said *Ella*, welcomed us and offered us help.

"I'm so sorry that you didn't get further," Ella shook Ten's hand. "That last goal was wrong, it should never have been allowed. Poor Stan was steamrollered."

He gave her an autograph and chatted for a while as I slunk over to the paint aisle with my anonymous-self blending in with a multitude of color cards and paint cans.

I located the lemon fast and added that and all the extra bits, rollers, trays, into the cart. I was halfway through checking the suitability and toxicity of various gloss paints when someone stumbled into me. I glanced up, expecting an apology, but a big bear of a man was looming over me, a can of paint in his hand and a nasty, twisted expression on his face.

"Call yourself a fucking team?" he shouted, his breath nothing more than fumes. "Fucking no one can shoot straight on your fucking rainbow shit, no wonder you let a pissant team mess you up sideways. Too busy fucking in the locker room."

I attempted to de-escalate and step back a little, but I was trapped between the cart and the paints and the drunk man, and realized the only way to deal with this was to gather myself, and pull all my NHL experience to the fore. I tilted my chin, drew back my shoulders, and decided that silk-covered steel diplomacy was the best way to go.

"If you could please move, sir." I added the honorific even though what I wanted was to shove a fist in his face. *Respect first, even in the face of bigotry.*

He loomed again, snarling, and I readied myself to hip check him the fuck away from me, but he abruptly sprawled on the floor, and Ten was there, a security guard in front of him. Ten's expression was focused, and he yanked the cart away and stood between me and the incoherent shouts from the man on the floor.

"You okay?" he asked, his tone urgent.

"Yeah, I'm okay. He's drunk."

"He's a fucking asshole," Ten muttered and turned to

head, where I didn't know, maybe to sit on my adversary, who knew? I grabbed his arm and held him.

"It's okay, Ten, nothing we haven't dealt with before."

Ten rounded on me, his eyes narrowed, a ferocious expression on his face.

"We shouldn't have to!" he snapped. "Charlotte shouldn't have to."

And I didn't have anything to say, because he was right.

Chapter Six

TEN

October

It had been a month since the showdown with the bigot at the paint store, yet it lingered at the fringes of my mind. While I was on the ice the worry stayed in the shadows, but when I lay in bed at night next to my husband, the concern returned. What kind of intolerant world were we bringing Charlotte into? Were Jared and I being selfish not to consider that aspect of our desire to have a child?

The worry dogged me, robbing me of rest, the whispers growing louder with each passing day. And since I couldn't stay on the ice twenty-four seven, I spent a lot of time stressed—until the day of our first game against Philly.

We arrived in the City of Brotherly Love around noon, the train ride less than two hours. Trent had made us reservations at his favorite French bistro on Walnut Street. Over a late lunch where I'd picked at my warm shrimp salad, I fell back into mulling over the future.

"Why are you not clapping?" Stan asked, driving an elbow into my side.

I grunted, dropped my fork, and applauded whatever had just taken place at the table. Dieter and Trent were kissing each other.

"What happened?" I asked on a whisper.

"They have set wedding date," Stan replied, his dark eyebrows knotted. Then he stood. All eyes flew to him. "I have much gas in my bowels from oysters. We will walk and make seafood toots outside."

With that, I was hoisted out of my seat and led out into a chilly Philadelphia afternoon.

"Come walk. I wish to see Liberty Bell." Stan steered me along, his mouth running constantly as we rounded Franklin Square. "This park is planned by the famous William Penn who our great state is named after. There is big statue of William on top of the city hall. He wants for Pennsylvania to be free state for all religions and minorities."

"Shame people forgot those principles," I muttered.

Stan made a sound in his throat then continued regaling me with American history. He knew more about his new country than I did, and I'd been born and schooled in the States.

We found the Liberty Bell and I took several pictures of him standing in front of it and a few of both of us for social media. Layton would be pleased.

"I send to children. We are discussing Revolutionary War much since seeing *Hamilton*," he said as we meandered to a nearby bench and took a seat.

"That's cool." I sat there for a bit watching Stan

interact with his children online. He grinned at me after Noah gave us a rousing rendition of "Right Hand Man" with Mama and the elder two kids providing the *booms* of the cannons.

"What is making you so sad and hating the shrimp?" he asked, ending his call home then lifting his eyes to drink in Independence Hall.

"I just…" I blew out a breath. "It's this place. The world. How do you justify bringing kids into such a hate-filled place?"

He nodded gently. "Is natural to worry. I think often of the climate change problem. Erik and I also see the hate at times."

I twisted on the bench to stare at his placid profile. "How do you not freak out over it? How do I justify bringing a child into a world so filled with toxicity? I just… I feel like I was selfish to do this."

"No, you are not selfish. You and Jared are loving couple, wishing for a child. Procreation is natural drive. To wish to have a child is good, strong, it makes families. And families are the strength and backbones for fighting against the bad things. Perhaps Charlotte will be the one who discovers how to clean the air, or cure cancer, or a million other things that will make our world happy place. Our children, they are our hope for a better future, yes?"

I thought on that long and hard then nodded. "Yeah, they are."

"There will always be people who hate, but if we fill the world with enough love, then we win! Oh! A soft pretzel man! I must have some!" He shot up off the bench and thundered over to the dude passing by with his rolling pretzel cart. Five minutes later we were making our way back to Walnut Street, chewing on soft pretzels, and discussing all the marvelous things that Charlotte would do to help save the planet.

"I think she will team up with Noah and make massive big plant that filters water for poor countries, and also set up a shelter for abandoned goats."

"Pollution control and goat rescue. Yeah, I can see that for our kids. Hey, Stan, thanks, man. Talking about it with you, well, it helped."

He smiled down at me. "You are welcomed. What are best friends for if not to make a dark day sunny with pretzels and goat talk?"

What indeed?

That night we arrived home on a high. We'd beaten Philly handily, my worries over the world while not gone were considerably lessened, and I'd managed to get my first hat trick of the season. Still feeling the effects of the adrenalin rush from the game, I pounced on Jared the moment he got through the front door. He gasped in shock when my mouth crashed down over his. He tasted of the coffee he'd had on the train ride home. I licked and lapped at his mouth, grinding my dick against his, and pulled his suit jacket off without breaking the wet kiss.

"Hat trick horniness," he chuckled when we stumbled into our bedroom a few minutes later, our clothes scattered behind us like a trail of breadcrumbs.

"Yeah, sort of, and other stuff. You're still the most beautiful man I've ever seen. Can I fuck you?" I rubbed against him, hot flesh to hot flesh, cock to cock, my hands slipping around him to cup that sweet ass of his. Jared didn't bottom often, that was usually at my request because I loved the feel of him filling me, but every so often I wanted to top the man. Was it tied to a hat trick?

"I'd love that," he replied, steering us to the bed. We tumbled into the thick, firm mattress, legs and arms tangled, lips seeking skin. I sucked a dark mark on his shoulder then pushed at him to roll over. "You really are in a mood tonight."

"Mm, yeah, three goals in one game and I'm Tony the Top. Jesus Jared, your ass is a work of art."

I grabbed both cheeks and squeezed while making my way closer to him on my knees. My thumbs skimmed his hole. He groaned. My dick kicked and I grabbed it at the base just in case it thought it was done. It was far from done, and it had better realize that. I laid over him, pressing him into the mattress, and kissed his shoulders and throat as I humped away madly. My cock sliding over his hole made him cuss and shudder.

"Ten, shit, get in me."

"Ah, man, I love hearing you say that." I nipped at his shoulder, pushed up, and jerked him back to his hands and knees. He reached for the nightstand then tossed me the lube. Licking my lips as I eyed his ass, I slathered lube over my cock then used two slick fingers to open him up. He rocked back, his blond head down, his powerful thighs easing his ass onto those digits so far in him.

My cock was leaking pre-cum. I withdrew my fingers, nudged his knees apart with mine, and settled myself right where I needed to be. Hips flat to his ass, my cock eased into him in one slippery thrust.

"Ah, shit!" he growled, rising from his elbows to slam himself backwards. My eyes rolled back. I grabbed his hips and pounded him across the bed and into the wall. When my balls drew up, he was spread over the headboard, his cheek against the wall, his cock spurting. His ass grabbed my cock, milking it as I blew apart inside him. "Ten, ah shit...yes..."

"Mm," I replied. Words weren't happening yet. I leaned up, got another quarter of an inch, and let my eyes drift shut as I emptied myself in his heat. When the last of the tremors eased, I pressed my lips to the back of his neck then eased out, taking just a second to enjoy the sight of my spunk leaking out of him.

Then I fell face first into the bed while he slipped off to clean up. "Sorry about that wet spot on your pillow," he called just as my face hit the goose down.

"Oh, dude, come on! Really?" I muttered and patted my pillow. Finding no wet spot, I called him a jerk of the highest caliber then buried my face into my pillow as a man should after fucking his spouse into the wall. Like, *literally* fucking him into the wall. I had a big, proud moment.

"Did you really think that I'd come all over your pillow?" he asked a moment later, dropping a wet washcloth to my head.

I reached up, pulled it off my hair, and rolled to my back to enjoy the sight of him picking up our clothes. "No, I guess not. It's not like you're me or something," I teased and got a soft over-the-shoulder smile. Then he moaned when he bent over to pick up a sock. "You okay? Nothing slipped out of place from that robust fucking from your stud of a younger husband? No hip breakage?"

"Oh please, do go fuck yourself," he countered then straightened and whipped my underwear at me. That made me chuckle. "I'm fine but thank you for your concern. The floor just seems to get further away every year."

"It's okay, I still think you're sexy AF. Bend over again so I can check out your ass one more time, won't you?"

"The next ass that gets checked out will be yours." He dropped our clothes into the hamper as my dick stirred. "And I'll make sure your face is smashed into a wall."

"Name the place, babe," I said while I wiped off my dick then flung the wet cloth toward the hamper. It missed. He harrumphed and picked it up, and I got that last look at his ass and balls. Such a fine sight.

"So, what did you and Stan talk about during your little walk to the Liberty Bell?" He pulled on some clean underwear then padded over to the bed as I lay there gawking at him. "What? You think that just because we coaches don't go to the team meals we don't know what's happening? Trent and Dieter have finally set a date for next July and are flying to the Philippines for the honeymoon."

"Oh cool! I kind of missed all that," I confessed as I eased the covers up over me.

"So I heard. Want to talk to me about it?" He crawled in next to me.

I snuggled into his side, my cheek on his chest. God, he was warm and firm. I loved how the gold curls on his chest tickled my nose.

I dropped an arm over his belly. "I was stressing about the future. Charlotte, the world, global warming, anti-LGBTQ rhetoric, you name it. That guy at the paint store accosting you like that really stirred something up, deep down."

"I can understand that. When someone threatens someone you love, it's frightening." His fingers skimmed the shell of my ear. It was dark outside, the house was quiet, and we were wrapped in each other's arms after making love. Hands down, this was one of my beloved times. Just Jared and me, cuddled close, the smell of sex and his cologne on the air…utter perfection.

"Yeah, it scared me, and kind of stunned me. I'd gotten complacent, I guess. Most of the hate and shit at the games has died down over the years. Sure, there are still a few assholes, but overall the fans know I'm there to play. Who I sleep with is inconsequential. They're learning, slowly as shit, but they are learning. Then that jerkwad shows up out of nowhere and brings all that shit back. And now we have a baby coming in two months. And that hate…will it be directed at her? When she grows up, will she be harangued for being what she is? Will the world still be like it is now? I just… it began to swallow me up."

"Why didn't you come to me about your worries?" He sounded hurt. Fuck me. I pushed up to rest my head on my hand, his gaze locking with mine. Such beautiful blue eyes.

"I don't know, honestly, I don't." He made that face he always made when I said something he didn't like. His eyebrows knit and his lips turn into a papercut. "Maybe I didn't want to bring you down with my stupid head stuff."

"Tennant, your head stuff is *not* stupid."

"No, well, yeah, I know. And not my head injury stuff, just the freak-out stuff." He studied me silently. "I don't know. Maybe I thought you wouldn't get my concerns because you'd fathered Ryker so long ago and couldn't relate to the problems this world and my generation are facing."

"I can see that. It's total horseshit, but I can see that. Yes, things were different twenty-five years ago. But we had worries back then, just different ones. Ten, every parent worries. It's what a parent does. You'll see. It starts at the moment of conception and ends... well, it ends when they put you in the ground. I still fret over Ryker, the world he lives in, him marrying a man and the hard times that may bring him. The world is never safe, and our children are going to face some mighty hard times, just as we did and our parents before us but they will face those challenges and they will overcome them. I have great faith in the younger generation. They're so woke."

That made me snigger. "'Woke' coming from you is just so funny, but yeah, I get what you mean." I kissed his crinkled brow. "Stan said that kids are the future and the hope."

"Mm, well, he's right. Charlotte will do amazing things."

"Yeah, she will. That girl will take the world by storm! I can see her now, facing down some corporate polluter or some bigot, shoulders back, chin high, strong and brave as Zena or RBG. Maybe she'll be a badass warrior Supreme Court justice!"

"That I can see happening." He smiled then so I kissed

him softly on the mouth. His phone started buzzing and we both scowled at it. He reached to his nightstand then fell back into the bed. I wiggled in tight, the post-sex stupor falling over me as he answered the call. My eyelids were lead and my body now craved sleep.

"Eddie, hello it's—Oh no. Okay, yes, we'll be right there."

My eyes flew open. Jared kicked off the covers. "What?" I asked, fear shoving away the happy vibes I'd been wrapped in.

"We have to get to the hospital. Isobel is in labor."

No. Oh shit. No. God no, not our baby.

Chapter Seven

JARED

With Ten driving, we made it to the hospital in record time, and in the fifteen minutes it took to get from our house to Mercy we were silent and battling our own fears. I didn't want to voice the worst scenario. The one where maybe we were losing our daughter, or that Isobel was in danger. What if something happened to Isobel? It would be our fault, and Eddie and the kids would be destroyed.

What have we done? Who do we think we were to imagine we deserve anything as beautiful as a daughter? Why did we even name her?

Why did we invest so much of *us* into something that could go horribly wrong?

Oh God. My chest cramped, but I didn't let any one single breath of pain escape because giving voice to any of it might have made it real. We were in that empty place where we knew nothing at all, and part of me wanted to stay there even as I needed to know what was happening. Ten was twitchy and tense, his jaw set, but at least he had the driving to think about, and it was only when we parked and he didn't move from his seat that the dam broke on his emotions.

"Fuck," he cursed, his hands curled so hard around the steering wheel that his knuckles were white. "We shouldn't have done it, what if—?"

"We have to stop," I interrupted him, and he stared at me, his eyes wide, and the fear in them was worse than when he'd thought his career was over. "We don't know anything yet. Let's be calm, go in, and be the best we can be for Isobel and Eddie." I didn't know if I could do any of that, but I was the voice of common sense. Not that it lasted long.

He shuddered, then unpeeled his fingers from the wheel and clenched and unclenched his fists; he was as lost in fear as me. After a few moments he killed the engine and removed his seatbelt, before inhaling, then exhaling, sharply.

"Okay."

I reached for his hand and held it tight. "Everything will be okay." I lied.

He nodded but didn't call me on my lie, or ask me how in hell I could know anything at all. How had we gone from love and passion to despair in such a flash of time?

We headed into the main hospital, knowing which way we had to go, taking the stairs instead of the elevator by unspoken agreement, and arriving at the fourth floor, both winded at the speed we'd moved. For me it was because I wasn't as fit as I'd been when I played, for Ten it was sheer agitation and fear. We paused a moment before pressing the buzzer for entrance, and as if he'd been waiting for us, Eddie popped up like a Jack-in-a-Box with an administrative by his side, and he let us in. He already had passes for us, which we slipped over our heads.

One of us should ask what was happening, and I began to speak, but he held up a hand.

"This way and we can talk," he said.

We followed him down the corridor, and through the last door on the left which led into a family room and as soon as the door shut Eddie turned to face us. He looked pale, exhausted, and I wanted to hug him so hard.

"Is Isobel okay?" Ten asked when I faltered.

"She's fine," Eddie began. "Her waters broke, and she has an infection, and they had to do a C-Section, I'm sorry you couldn't be here—"

"Wait, Charlotte is here already?" I blurted, not quite believing what I was hearing.

"And she's okay?" Ten added, just as fast.

"The doctor will want to talk to you."

What did that mean? Why wasn't he telling us about our daughter? Was something horribly wrong? I swayed into Ten, and my legs felt as if they were going to give way, and I'd fall in a heap on the floor.

A woman stepped inside and consulted notes as she closed the door behind her.

"Mr. and Mr. Madsen-Rowe?" she asked.

"Here," I said.

"Us," Ten murmured at the same time. He squeezed my hand hard, and I wanted to be the strong one but any minute now I was going to lose my shit.

"My name is Doctor Grierson, I was on call when Mrs. Mackie was brought in after her water broke early, with a suspected infection and that unfortunately entailed we had to perform an emergency—"

"Oh God," Ten groaned.

"Mrs. Mackie is well."

"Her husband, Eddie, he told us that," Ten finished.

"Where is our daughter?" I asked and the doctor wasn't at all fazed by my rudeness.

"She's in the NICU, I'll take you there."

I glanced at Eddie with worry.

"Will you be okay?" I asked.

Eddie smiled. "We're fine. Now go see your baby, I'm going to be with Izzy."

Nothing made sense, all concept of politeness flew out the window. As soon as I knew Eddie was going to be okay with Isobel, I hustled Ten and the doctor out of the door, aware that no one was moving fast enough. Doctor Grierson didn't push back, and we moved out of the maternity ward and through double doors to the NICU. Charlotte wasn't supposed to be in there, she was supposed to be safe inside Isobel for another four weeks. I wracked my brains—how bad was it for a child to be born at thirty-six weeks? Was that even a thing to worry about? Why couldn't I recall everything I'd read? Why was my mind a complete blank?

We had to put on scrub aprons, and masks, and then we followed the doc inside a hot space that I had prayed we'd never have to see.

"Mr. and Mr. Madsen-Rowe, this is your daughter."

She moved to one side, revealing a nurse checking readouts, and all I could focus on was the glass and the baby inside. A tube into her nose, small pads on her chest, and fluff on her tiny head, she was perfect and small, and my breath left me in a sharp exhale.

"Oh my god," Ten murmured, and stepped closer to the unit, dragging me with him. I hadn't even realized I'd stopped dead in one spot, but we were still a few paces away. The NICU was like a NASA control room, the heat a slap in the face, flashing lights and beeping monitors everywhere, and I had no idea what some of the things in here did. We'd toured, but I never imagined we'd have to be in here, and I didn't know enough.

Why don't I know more?

Charlotte was at the center of a tangle of tubes and wires, and a wave of both grief and love passed over me.

"It's expected that you will feel overwhelmed, but I'm pleased to say that your daughter weighed in at five and a half pounds," the doctor said.

"Charlotte," Ten interjected. "Her name is Charlotte." The tag simply said Baby Madsen-Rowe, and somehow that seemed very wrong. She was Charlotte and Ten was just the first one of us to say it. The doctor wasn't upset, if anything she softened and her voice lowered it a little.

"Even though Charlotte looks healthy we need to monitor her for some of the unfortunate problems of prematurity. Not that this appears to be an issue; all the signs are good."

The doctor's voice was white noise, as I stared down at our perfect tiny Charlotte. I wish Ryker had been there so he could meet his sister, I expected we'd have hours to wait, that anyone who wanted to be with us could be, but standing here with Ten I felt as if we were the only two men in the entire world.

"…lungs won't be completely developed for another couple of weeks, and also, she doesn't have enough fat to stay warm or enough strength to breast or bottle-feed effectively. Your surrogate has donated the first…."

Oh my god. She's perfect. I refuse to let anything ever hurt her.

"…continuing to protect their health until they are ready to go home is important. There are no signs currently of respiratory issues. She's not hypoglycemic, and we're keeping her warm and as unstressed as we can as she fights."

"She's fighting?" Ten sounded broken.

"Life is always a fight," the nurse said with a smile. How could she smile? What did she think was happening here? Our daughter was bright red, covered in fine down; she wasn't the healthy bouncy baby we'd planned for, she was struggling and I couldn't do a damn thing to help, and… *I'm losing my shit.*

"…Charlotte's heart rate was faster than normal and with the possibility of infection—"

"What's wrong with her heart?" I interrupted, fear gripping me. What if she had the same issues as me? It wasn't as if I was her biological dad, but that didn't mean she could be the one in a million who wasn't born with a defect in her tiny fragile body.

"Nothing, Jared, it's okay, listen to me." Ten was cradling my face. "Look at me, Jared. You're in panic mode, come back to me." He'd clearly been listening. "Doc was saying that they had to do the C-section. She's fine, the doc says she's doing well, and her heart is strong."

I sagged into Ten for a moment, and he held me up, and then I did what every new father had to do if they wanted to be strong. I pulled myself together, and hoped to hell the adrenalin rush would subside before I was sick. I couldn't breathe behind the mask, and more than anything I wanted to touch Charlotte, to make sure she was real. Love was starting to push shock aside, and the doc kept talking about times and dates, reassuring us that the nurse, Sarah-Louise, would be on hand for anything we needed to ask.

"When can we take her home?" Ten was asking serious questions, and I was standing there like an idiot.

"All being well, we would hope in around two weeks, of course we will carefully monitor the situation, and in partnership with the healthcare…"

I touched the glass gently, my entire world focused on Charlotte, lying there in that nest of bedding and wires, her tiny chest rising and falling, her hands so small, her long legs still bent from being inside Isobel, slightly on her side facing us, her eyes closed and her lashes fanned on her cheek. I swear even as we stood there that her color was better, and that she seemed less fragile.

"If you have any further questions, then I'm a phone call away."

I recalled shaking the doctor's hand, I knew that we thanked her, and the nurse, and I remembered Eddie coming in and explaining that Isobel was well, and so thankful that everything had turned out okay.

Other than that, it was me, Ten, and Charlotte against the world, and nothing was going to separate me from this fierce love that I felt for the tiny scrap of a baby that moved inside the incubator.

She was already in my heart, right alongside Ryker and Ten, and abruptly, my heart was full.

On day three we were able to hold Charlotte in what the nurse called Kangaroo care. Ten went first, sitting in the chair next to the incubator as the monitoring wires couldn't be removed.

"So if you unbutton your shirt," the midwife said, and Ten undid the whole thing right to the bottom. He'd already washed his hands, and only just showered at home, and I could see the shakiness in his hands as the nurse pressed a miniature cap onto Charlotte's head and then placed her directly against Ten's bare chest. "Skin-to-skin is best," Sarah-Louise explained, "so if you could support the weight of her, here and here." She moved Ten's hands to the right position and he did exactly what he'd been told.

"She's light as air," Ten whispered, and glanced up at me, his green eyes bright with tears. "And so warm."

Sarah-Louise patted his shoulder. "Then if we close your shirt over her, you can lean back and relax with your daughter."

Selfishly, I didn't want to lose the beautiful sight of my husband cradling our Charlotte, but he didn't move as Sarah-Louise crossed over the material. I sat on the chair next to him, scooting it around so we could talk, and so I could see Charlotte's tiny face just over the top of Ten's shirt. She was fast asleep, her belly full, her lungs strong, and her heart whole.

"I'll be back in a minute," Sarah-Louise offered a soft smile, and moved away to the next machine where fellow parents were in a vigil over their son. That left Ten and me with Charlotte, and even in this space-aged room with the beeps and the lights, we felt alone.

"Jared," Ten murmured, and I placed my hand over the top of his shirt. "I didn't know."

"Didn't know what?"

Ten cleared his throat. "I didn't know I could love someone so completely in such a short time."

"I know."

We sat in silence for a while. "Was it like this with Ryker?" Ten broke the silence with his softly spoken question.

I nodded, recalling that first moment I'd seen Ryker as a baby. He hadn't been in NICU, he'd been sturdy, strong, crying and wailing with a healthy pair of lungs, and I'd fallen completely in love.

"I remember telling Ryker's mom that I would kill anyone who hurt a hair on his head." I huffed a laugh at that. "Now look at him."

"I can't imagine Ryker being this small."

"He was born at nine pounds, always seemed so strong."

"Charlotte is strong." Ten's expression was utterly determined.

"So strong."

And the next day it was my turn to hold her, and my

whole word shifted with the weight of love that filled my heart.

Charlotte was in the NICU for eleven days, and somehow we fit staying by her in and around hockey.

The Railers management gave me some allowance in the schedule for being with her, but I still had to be there for games, and Ten got virtually no allowance at all. Despite the Railers' support of family, he was the star of the team and we were at the start of the season. Against all the odds, Ten kept his head in the game to such an extent that the Railers had had three games in that space of time and we'd won them all. Every single skater on the ice rallied around and I don't think I'd seen such focus before; if we could've bottled it, we'd be lifting the cup this year.

Every other second away from hockey we were at the hospital, either in the NICU with Charlotte until she could go home, or taking turns to nap in the family room. On the odd occasion when exhaustion became too much, we would sit together in that room, and lean on each other for support, and the morning they told us we could take her home, we sat there together and hugged so hard we couldn't breathe.

"I love you," Ten said, and buried his face in my neck. "And I love Charlotte."

"I love you, too." I held him tight. "I love you both."

Chapter Eight

TEN

"Are you sure she's okay lying like that?" I glanced from Charlotte to my mother. Jared was downstairs on the phone with Ryker talking about the latest snag in the wedding plans. Wedding plans were as unpredictable as babies. Just when a guy thought things were all set everything suddenly got twisted upside down. "I'm not sure she should be sleeping like that. What if the mobile comes loose and falls on her face?"

"Tennant, darling, my sweet youngest boy, trust me on this, Charlotte is perfectly safe on her back." She pulled the yellow duvet up to my daughter's chin.

"Are you sure? I thought they said…" I ran a hand through my hair. My head was so full of newborn information that I was beginning to feel concussed. "No, okay, yeah, you're right. Back to sleep. Right. Sorry. I didn't mean to question your expertise."

She patted my arm. "It's fine. Things have changed a lot since I was putting you and your brothers down for the night, but I've kept up. After all, with all the grandkids coming along, Dad and I had to stay up-to-date. Why don't you go grab a smoothie before you go play? You look haggard."

I did? "Haggard? Nah, I'm just… nervous. Why didn't they give us a manual at the hospital? What if she gets sick? She's so tiny. Are they sure she should be home with us? I'm… yeah…" I took a deep breath. "I'm mildly freaking out. Maybe I should skip the game tonight."

"Go play hockey. Tennant, I got this." She patted Charlotte's tummy then turned to look up at me. "I have all the numbers for all the doctors in Harrisburg and all the surrounding counties."

"That was Jared," I was quick to point out. She smiled. "I might have added the poison control center and the medical helicopter numbers, but all the doctors were Jared."

"Go play hockey. Everything will be fine. This isn't my first rodeo."

That made me smile. "You're the rootinest tootinest grandmother west of the Pecos."

"Darn tootin', partner. Now go to work before you get fined for being late."

"Someone will call between periods, just to check." She pointed at the nursery door; her eyes merry. "Right, yeah, I'm going. Thanks for filling in until we can decide on a nanny. We thought we'd have more time but… well, Charlotte was in a hurry to make her debut."

"I'm more than happy to help out. I did it for Jamie's Lisa when they had their last baby. That's the joy of being newly retired."

I pressed a kiss to her soft cheek, then leaned over the

rail of the crib and dusted a kiss to Charlotte's sweetly-scented dark hair.

"See you in a few hours, buttercup." Her tiny lips fluttered at the sound of my voice. I fell more deeply in love than I'd been the last time I'd looked at her. "She's the most beautiful baby in the world."

Mom rubbed my back as she moved up beside me. "I agree, but grandmas tend to be biased. Go get Jared."

"I'm here. Oh my God, weddings! I told them to just elope," Jared said as he rushed into the nursery, his tie in his hand and his shirt collar standing up.

"No, you didn't," I replied, moving to let him wiggle in to admire our daughter sleeping.

"Okay no, but I was close. I don't recall us having all these creative differences when we got married." He pecked Charlotte's cheek then gave my mother a quick hug. "We have to go or we'll be late. Jean, thank you, for everything. I promise we'll get the nanny situation taken care of by the end of the week if not sooner."

"Oh posh, don't rush. I'm in my glory. Now *go!*" She shooed us out of our own child's room.

Jared and I exchanged an amused look then raced to the car and sped to the barn. We chatted about Charlotte, of course, and Ryker's wedding planning battles. It seemed he and Jacob had differing views on where to have their upcoming nuptials. Once we walked inside the East River Arena, our minds switched gears. Hockey became the most important thing. But even as I taped my stick and pulled on my shoulder pads, Charlotte was never far from my thoughts.

We were squaring off against Buffalo tonight. They

were always a tough team, heavy on defense, with some monstrously big men looking to knock me over the boards. I'd gotten used to the defensive attention over the years. Things started out smooth, a little awkward to be honest. We'd not played Buffalo since last April. They'd gotten a new goalie, Jens Hedlund, who used to play with the Railers during our first two years. He'd been traded and Bryan had taken his spot as Stan's backup. Jens was a rangy Swede who sat in his crease like an owl, big dark gaze flitting around, waiting to pounce on a puck instead of a mouse.

The first period was spent feeling out Jens. We had all kinds of info on him, but he'd refined his stance, and was now much faster with his glove hand. He liked to play the puck, and he was good at it, plus he was prone to being mouthy.

"Okay, just saying, Jens is a jerk," Adler complained during a TV timeout.

"Ignore him," I said as Jared was yelling something at the defense. I washed out my mouth, spit the water to the ice, and crammed my mouthguard back in.

"Right, totally ignoring him," Adler replied, tossed his water bottle to a trainer, and then skated off to torment Jens. "Hey! Headly! Got any ideas where Mongo is? Oops, wait! I found him!"

I chuckled when he draped an arm around Mills Bates, a huge D-man, last-of-the-grinders kind of guy. Mills called Adler various crude names as I skated in to take the face off. My eyes met the Buffalo center, a nice guy named Rory Biggleston, aka Biggy. The puck hit the ice at the same time Mills' and Adler's gloves did. I whipped the puck to Connor but the play kind of fizzled as everyone on the ice opted to get into a fight instead of playing hockey.

I skated over to the crowd, pulled on the back of Mills' sweater, and managed to get him off Adler. He took a swing at me. Connor jumped in, and before I knew it I was on my back, head ringing.

Whistles were blowing, and our head trainer was hovering over me as I pushed Mills off and, slow and steady, got to my skates.

"I'm good, I'm fine," I chanted over and over, but I was still led off the ice and into a dark room. Which, yeah, given my head issues, was the right call but still…

Jared appeared in the doorway ten or so minutes later.

"Hey," he said as I sat there sipping ginger ale and singing the state capitals song a la Wakko from *Animaniac's* fame.

"He's good," the team doctor said to my husband. "Just remember that if you start to feel any symptoms—"

"Yep, I'll shout," I replied, feeling like a fool. Once it was just Jared and me in the medical office, I gave him a weak smile. "First thing, I am really okay. It was just a bump so you can stop looking at me that way."

He rubbed his face and when he was done he did look less tight. "Sorry, but every time I see you go down and your head hits the ice…"

I leaned in to steal a quick kiss. "I know. So hey, instead of worrying about me, call home and see how Charlotte is."

"She's fine. Jean is an old hand with new babies," he said while staring at me as if I was about to drop over.

"Stop it, I'm fine." I waved at his narrowed eyes. "I think we should call."

"You know how coach is about cell phone use during a game," he replied, easing back a bit to allow me to slip down from the exam table. "Plus we have to learn to manage the worry in a productive way. We can't be calling home every twenty minutes; it'll drive the nanny nuts and make us paranoid."

"Yeah, right, I know I just…man this parental concern stuff is rough."

"You have no clue. Just wait until she learns to drive."

"Oh God above…"

The following day was a rare day off. No game or morning skate. The cold winds of early November were blowing, a cold front roaring in over Pennsylvania from Canada. The perfect day to whittle down the fifteen candidates from four top-notch nanny organizations in Harrisburg. Mom, Jared, and I spent the whole day interviewing people, men and women, for the position. When dinner time rolled around we were seated in the living room, with pizza and soda, staring blankly at each other.

"I just didn't see anyone in that batch that reflects the type of woman I want to see taking care of Charlotte," Jared stated, while giving our daughter a bottle. She was a voracious eater, which helped to put us at ease.

"So it has to be a woman?" I enquired then took a massive bite of the slice of pizza I'd guided to my mouth.

"Well, no…" Jared floundered a bit as Charlotte sucked noisily on her special preemie nipple. Mom chuckled at his discomfort while nibbling on a crust she'd swiped off my plate. "Okay, maybe. Yes, I know, I'm being sexist but I just feel better with a woman taking care of her. An older woman, say in her sixties, who dresses modestly and cooks well."

"Mm, so you want Mrs. Doubtfire?" I tossed out and got a dark look from my husband.

"If you add British to that list we could possibly call Mary Poppins, although she's younger and comes with chimney sweeps and dancing penguins, which is something to consider," Mom said glibly.

I snorted so hard my sinuses vibrated.

Jared huffed, placed the half empty bottle to his thigh, and eased Charlotte up to his shoulder. He really was a natural. I always felt so clumsy and ham-fisted when I was holding her, but Jared was just so at ease. Maybe that came with experience.

"You're both hilarious. I see where you get your sarcasm gene, Tennant." Mom inclined her head. "Now that you mention it our chimney could use a good sweeping."

"Well, just for the record, Ryker tells me that Colorado has a male nanny and he's great with his baby," I threw out then took another bite of pizza. I'd have to do double the miles on the treadmill tomorrow but it would be worth it.

"Colorado is sleeping with his male nanny," Jared pointed out right as Charlotte burped a tiny little "Eep" of a burp that made me feel all fuzzy inside. It was like hearing a kitten burp. Damn, she was cute!

"I promise I won't sleep with the male nanny if we choose him," I said with a wink.

Jared tossed me a look. "I'll make the same vow if we hire a woman, which I think we should."

"Tsk, tsk, your antiquated gender norms are showing," I replied around the food in my mouth.

"Tennant, don't speak with your mouth full," Mom chided then sighed. "Why don't we focus less on the sex of the applicants and more on their credentials? Give me another slice. No, a skinny one. That one there with the extra pepperoni." She pointed. I gave Mom a raised eyebrow. "You sound like your father. I won't have heartburn." She held out her plate, so I gave her the skinny slice.

"We could sleep on it for a few days," Jared offered then eased Charlotte down to see if she wanted more bottle. She did and latched on as if she'd not eaten in a week. I loved how they looked together, Charlotte resting in the crook of his arm in her Elvis jumpsuit sleeper, courtesy of Stan's boxes of clothes. It was a little big on her, obviously, but he'd asked if we'd found it so we'd dressed her in it and sent pictures. The Russian was so moved he'd gotten teary. "Give it some time to simmer and reconvene."

"No, Jared, we don't have time to dick around. Sorry, Mom." She flicked my ear and gave me a firm tsking. "We're leaving for a Canadian road trip in three days. We have to pick one now. Give them time to get here and moved into the guest room. Mom will chill with them for a week or two, to supervise, and then when we come home we'll make it full-time if all goes well."

Jared mulled over that in silence, his gaze resting on

Charlotte who had fallen asleep while eating. Mom and I looked at each other as he ruminated.

"I really liked Candace," Mom said when it looked as if we might've been sitting there all night. "She was older, had a child, has taken all the required courses, and had a delightful sense of humor."

"I second Candace," I said then lifted a crust into the air to make the seconding official. "She's perfect. Widowed..." Mom flicked my ear again. "Ouch! Shit. Sorry, crap. I didn't mean being widowed was perfect, that was tragic, but she's not married and her son is grown. I think fifty is a good age for a nanny. She's not going to be dating all the time and her grandma nurturing emotions will be...what?"

"You make it sound like a woman of fifty is ready for the nursing home," Mom scolded.

I looked to Jared for help but he wasn't offering any.

"Your ageist bias is showing," he whispered then sniggered as my mother chewed me out for saying a woman over forty was old and worn out, which I totally had not said but man, she sure heard it that way.

"Okay, okay, I take it back! She's not old and ready to be a grandma. She's vibrant and sexual. Cripes, I just meant that she was a good choice because she's mature and settled."

Mom glowered at me for a few seconds then flicked my ear for good measure.

"Jared, what do you think about Candace Perales?" Mom asked.

"She was fine, I just..." He pushed to his feet. "I'm going to put her down for the night."

"You mean for two hours," I teased and got a mealy smile from Jared before he climbed the stairs. Mom and I exchanged confused looks.

"Why don't you go talk to him and I'll clean up," she said as we watched him disappear into the shadows at the top of the stairs.

"Okay." I got up and followed Jared's steps into the nursery. He was pulling the rails up on the crib when I stepped up beside him. We stood there in silence watching our daughter sleep, my pinkie finger finding then curling around his.

"I hate the thought of leaving her alone. It's like Ryker all over again, only this time my child is going to be with a stranger. It was bad enough leaving my wife to take care of an infant alone, at least I knew and trusted her, but now I'm off again and entrusting someone I don't know to raise my child. All that old guilt is right here." He thumped his chest with his left hand. "Only compounded."

"So what are you saying? That you want to quit hockey and stay home with Charlotte? That I should quit and stay home with her?"

He shook his head, his jaw set, his blue eyes melancholy. "No, of course not, you can't quit. The team needs you."

"It needs you too." I let my weight shift to the left so my head would drop to his shoulder. The nightlight by the crib shone softly on Charlotte snoozing away. "We knew this was part of it when we decided to have her. The guilt, you even warned me about it."

"I know, it's just harder than I thought it would be. I assumed because I'd run this race before I'd be stronger. I was wrong. It's just as hard if not more so because this will be my last chance to do it right."

"Not necessarily, we could have another baby in a few years. And even if we don't, Jared, you're a fantastic father. Ryker loves you. He gets it, he understands that hockey is what we do."

"Yes, because he's a hockey player."

Yeah, that had some merit. "True, that helps, but who knows, maybe Charlotte will grow up and want to play hockey. Maybe she'll be the first woman hockey player who also serves on the SCOTUS! Don't laugh, I totally see her doing all kinds of incredibly impressive shit. Stuff. My mouth, honestly." I reached up to flick my own ear. Jared smiled over at me. "Honestly, we're going to fu—screw things up along the way because no one is a perfect parent but we love her *so* much. She'll know it, she'll feel it, and when we're gone she'll have that love all stored up inside, like a bank deposit vault that she can withdraw then fill back up when we're home."

"I didn't realize that love could be hidden away for later," he whispered, reaching down to trail his fingers along her cheek. "I like thinking of it that way."

I nodded then snuggled into his side. "I'm fucking eloquent. Shit! Damn! Crap. Sorry, Lottie. Ignore your father's foul hockey mouth."

He pressed a kiss to my hair. "I like Candace too. Let's call the agency and tell them we'd like her to come out for a few weeks on a trial basis."

"Cool. You go call. I have to wash my mouth out with soap."

Chapter Nine

JARED

November

"Is it just me, or does she seem a bit warm?" Ten cradled Lottie protectively, as if Doctor Grierson was about to whisk her away and never give her back.

The doc rechecked the paperwork that Ten had thrust at her in the hallway. "Her temperature is perfectly fine," she reassured him with a soft smile.

"I think maybe we should let Doctor Grierson go now." I tugged on Ten's arm to indicate that we needed to leave this poor woman alone, but he was *Ten*, and if Ten was one thing it was persistent, on and off the ice. We'd seen the healthcare specialist, spoken about weight and height and feeding and everything else on the list they went through. One month after leaving the hospital she was thriving and doing everything a baby should had it been born at full-term. Yes, Charlotte was on the fifteenth percentile on the charts, but she was sticking to that line like a statistician's dream.

We were leaving, everything was good, she'd passed with flying colors, and we were heading home for the rest of our day, which for me was off to the arena, and for Ten, conditioning in the home gym. We were so close to getting away but with the exit in sight *that* was the moment Ten spotted poor Doctor Grierson and just seeing her appeared to open the floodgates to every single worry Ten had been holding inside.

"Last week she wouldn't take her bottle, we tried everything, but she just batted it away as if she didn't want it, and she was fussy. We burped her, and then I walked her around the house for a while, and then she took the bottle, but what was that all about? Should we be worried?"

When Ten said he'd walked, he meant it, up and around the house, out into the big yard, complete circles, talking to Charlotte the entire time, and he didn't let me take over once, as if he was taking this entire childcare thing on his own shoulders. I was alternating between feeling as if Charlotte was going to be daddy's little princess, and worrying that Ten was losing his shit.

Case in point, accosting the esteemed childbirth expert to discuss an issue with feeding.

"It's okay, Doctor, she was fine," I told her as if she needed to know.

"Then she wouldn't sleep and I thought that maybe it was something I did. Should I not take her for a walk? Am I holding her wrong? She was due a feed at four, but she slept right through it, and it was four twenty-three before she woke up."

"Ten, she's fine," I reassured him.

Doctor Grierson checked her watch, and I cringed inside. I didn't want to take up her time; there could've been a baby that needed her help, and we shouldn't have been holding her back.

"Do you have five minutes to talk?" Doc asked.

Ten latched onto that with fear in his expression. "What's wrong?"

"Nothing," Doc smiled. "Follow me." Like chicks after a momma hen we followed her into a room with her name on the door, and she waited until we were inside before she closed it shut. "Can I see?" She held out her hands for Charlotte and Ten passed her over without hesitation. "I bet hockey is a hard game," she said, as if she wasn't holding a baby. Did she want an answer?

"It is," I answered, and Ten shot me a look of disbelief that I was continuing a conversation about hockey when Charlotte was supposed to be the focus.

Doc held Charlotte up and bussed a kiss to her belly, then sat on the couch, bouncing our tiny daughter gently on her knees. "All those men on sharp blades going at whatever miles an hour, hitting that plastic disc into a net."

"Rubber, vulcanized rubber," I corrected, and got another one of Ten's *looks*.

"It must take discipline, am I right? To learn to skate? Discipline, repetition and practice, but eventually it's second nature, I guess."

Ten nodded, but he was staring at Charlotte who made this small squeaky sound and clenched her tiny fist in Doc's hair.

"What's the best ever goal you've ever scored, Ten?"

Doc lifted Charlotte high. "You're so beautiful you sweet thing, look at you all cute and tiny. So yes, the best goal, Ten?"

The second time she worded the question it was more of a demand.

Ten snapped back. "Boston, March nineteen, up against my brother, he dropped his guard, I took a chance, and managed to hit the net."

"Is that right, Jared? Is that Ten's best goal?"

"Yeah, for sure. He was out of position, Brady was in his face, and Ten corralled the puck on his skate, kicked it through Brady's skates, collected it again, deked, passed by the other D, big guy, then avoided two forwards, before batting it out of the air and into the net."

"Did you practice that?" she asked, and unpeeled Charlotte's fingers from her hair with a chuckle.

"You can't," Ten murmured, and glanced up at me. "You can learn the individual parts, that's the repetition, but sometimes things just fall in place."

"Do your practices sometimes run over?"

"Why? Is that causing—?"

"Yes, they do," I interrupted before Ten got any paler.

"Is Charlotte okay?" Ten insisted.

Doc bounced her again. "Oh she's perfect, a tiny little miracle and a happy accident of genetics that made her. Just like you with hockey, her body is learning all the repetitions. The feeding, the sleeping, the way her muscles strengthen, and she sees the blur of shapes, it's all repetition. Sometimes it might not be perfect, but maybe she needed that extra twenty minutes' sleep because she was busy learning to see something in a dream. Or maybe her brain was processing a voice, or a scent. A baby doesn't do things on their daddies' say so."

"Oh," Ten murmured, and dipped his head. "You're saying that she's having to work hard, and I should stop worrying."

"It's the hardest thing in the world being a parent, and you have the added complication that you didn't carry your daughter. There is a disassociation that is there, but the best thing you can do for Charlotte is to love her the way you do, and keep loving her, until she's practiced enough in life, and then her future can be full of all kinds of miracles."

I leaned into Ten who pressed back. "Sorry," he murmured. "I'm being stupid—"

"You're not at all," Doc spoke with authority and Ten straightened. "Every parent is scared, it's nothing new, but Charlotte is thriving, and has two dads who love her so much that one of them is freaking out, and the other is pretending not to freak out."

She had me there. I'd spent so long balancing out Ten that all my fears and worries were buried deep.

Ten and I glanced at each other, and I sent him a rueful smile that he returned.

"I have to go," she said, but stole another kiss to Charlotte's cheek before she handed her back to Ten. "Be kind to yourselves." She showed us out, and locked her room behind her. "One thing though," she said, and patted my arm. "Watch out for Dallas next week, they're scrappy and gunning for Ten."

Then she sauntered away, ponytail bobbing, and it was just me and Ten in the hallway.

"We should give her a season ticket," I said.

"Two."

I tugged Ten in for a sideways hug, with Charlotte between us. "Let's go home."

Thanksgiving came around so fast, with Charlotte passing six weeks, chaos in our house, and today the first time that Ryker would meet his sister. The Raptors were in Pittsburgh, and that meant two whole days of Ryker driving over to stay with us, and Jacob flying east to join him. We'd already picked up Jacob who'd fussed over Charlotte as if she was the first baby he'd ever seen, but it was nothing compared to Ryker's reaction.

He arrived, and after the quickest hug ever, he headed past me into the house to find Charlotte, taking her from Ten and then dancing around the kitchen with her.

"She's so perfect." He pressed kisses to her head. "Hey, Lottie! I'm your big brother Ryker." He held her up so they were at eye level, "Ryker... big brother Ryker," he repeated this until she let out a tiny babbling squawk, and then laughed out loud and startled her. I watched him with Charlotte, Ten watching with an amused expression, and my entire world was right and perfect. Ryker already had three half-sisters after his mom remarried, and now he had four. Charlotte gripped one of his curls, tugging it to her mouth, but in a smooth move he removed it, and cradled her close to him. "Does she need a feed? Does she need her Uncle Ryker to feed her?"

Candace visited briefly, but today and tomorrow she was with family, and when she left it was with a Ryker jersey, because it turned out she was a Raptors fan. Although she put that down to her loving to watch dreamy Coach Carmichael. We'd not long gotten over that image when Jacob barreled into the kitchen, his hair wet from the shower.

"You're here!"

The kiss he and Ryker shared was enough to burn us all, and I extricated Charlotte and sat on the stool.

"Mom called," Jacob began.

"Not now," Ryker warned, and Jacob subsided. There was a layer of tension, and Ryker had already explained the two of them wanted different kinds of weddings. They'd planned it for Bye Week, which fell right across Valentine's Day, but nothing had gone smooth for them in decision-making. I recalled our wedding and the stress of it all, but these two needed someone to sit down and explain that it didn't matter what the day was like if you were next to the man you loved. Jacob sat next to me, and Ryker took Charlotte back, and did some more dancing, with Ten joining in, which deteriorated into a twerk-off right in front of us. Somehow in all of that, Charlotte dozed off in her big brother's arms, and all four of us ended up sprawled on our sofas.

Ten cuddled into my side, and I played with his hair as Ryker talked about the season, and peppered Charlotte with so many kisses that I thought she might wake up. She didn't. It seemed as if Ryker had a magic touch.

"And then Colorado put a bottle in the cubby, only the ass had replaced it with…"

I tuned out the stories of Colorado and his pranks, and how he was apparently more settled now, because it sounded as if he was still an unknown quantity in the locker room. He was lucky he was so skilled, because otherwise…

"And then Alex slid in the water, and it was some funny shi—stuff. Sorry, sis," he murmured, and allowed Jacob to take her from him.

Seeing Ryker, with his fiancé and a baby, had me feeling the warm and fuzzies, which is why I did something really ill-advised. "So, how goes the wedding?"

Ryker huffed. "We're agreeing to disagree on some of the finer details."

"We're agreeing?" Jacob seemed surprised to hear this.

"I want to invite the whole team, you want just family and friends, so I agree we cut down on who we invite."

"You know the only reason I want to keep it small is so we can afford it."

"I earn more than enough to pay for our wedding," Ryker murmured.

I couldn't believe my ears. He was still on a rookie contract but word was the Raptors were going to offer him a big contract to center the second line behind Tate, and that would be good money, but to blurt it out like that was offensive.

Jacob handed Charlotte to Ten who sat across from him, then stood and smoothed his jeans. I could see he was taking time to think about his words, and with measured calm he spoke in a low voice to Ryker. "And saying shit like that makes you an asshole." He stalked off, threw open the patio door, and headed out into the cold of the day.

"You want to explain what you just said, Ryker?" I

used my best dad voice, because I'd never heard such crap coming from my normally level-headed son.

He mumbled something.

"Ryker?"

Ten read the room, took himself out of the equation, citing Charlotte needing a feed, then it was just me and my idiot son.

"I don't know what I'm doing." Ryker sounded miserable as he hunched over his knees.

I scooted forward and pressed a hand to his back, just to reassure him that even if he was being an ass I was there to listen.

"Everyone gets cold feet—"

"It's not that."

"Do you not want to get married?"

He shot me a surprised glance. "Of course I do."

"Ryker, you know you can tell me anything, do you still love Jacob?"

"Yes, of course—"

I sighed, because Ryker was in a twist over something that was a lot more serious in his head than maybe it should be. "There's no *of course* about any of this, Ry. You threw what you earn in his face, as if it was a natural thing to do, and that's not like you, and I can't believe you even said that."

He groaned, "Shit, Dad. I don't know where to start."

"The beginning, and we'll try and work this out."

"It's just… he's started working on this project with a tech guy. Adam is a millionaire who made his money in environmental *whatever*. Adam wants to find a sustainable farming something or other, and tells me that Jacob is a handsome sexy genius at every turn. Jacob defends him, says it's all a big joke, but I'm…"

"Jealous? Confused? Lashing out?" He hunched even more, and I scooted closer so I could put an arm over his shoulder. "You know he loves you, you know there's nothing to worry about."

"I know, but it's the wedding. Adam offered us the use of his estate—his freaking estate—and I don't want another man doing that for us."

"Oh I see, so Jacob does want to use it?"

"No," Ryker sounded so miserable. "He doesn't. And that is the worst of it, because I don't even know what I'm messed up about."

Oh, my poor boy. He needed guidance here, but instead of saying how much Jacob loved him and how it would all be okay, I was firm.

"You owe Jacob an apology, Ry."

"I know."

"You love him, he loves you, I suggest you go out and talk to him. Take coats because it's cold out there."

"Yes, sir."

He trudged into the hall, then just as miserable, he walked back with coats in hand, and stopped at the door to the backyard. "Wish me luck."

"You don't need it, just be honest, and don't come back in until you've made it right."

"Sorry, Dad."

"It's okay."

"Love you."

I smiled at him then, softening my next words. "I love you too. Now go fix things."

As soon as the door shut behind Ryker, Ten popped back into the room, Charlotte in the crook of his arm sucking at a bottle.

"You're good at this dad stuff."

I crossed to him, kissed our daughter, and then kissed him. "So are you."

Epilogue

TEN

Christmas

Perfection.

That was the only word I could think of to describe our first Christmas with Charlotte. For the rest of the world the holiday seemed to be fraught, and yeah, there had been some crazy moments leading up to the big day. Like the night that Lottie had woken us up crying with a fever. A two a.m. run to the ER with me in a panic turned out to be just an ear infection, something that was common in kids, or so my brothers told me.

Then there was the family Zoom call, which included Ryker, about how we were sure we would love everything that Santa brought our daughter but we'd love it even more if it were gender-neutral. I even gave them links but I genuinely think they'd been expecting us to say that. They understood it was important to us to let Lottie grow up free of labels, so she could decide who she was and what she wanted to be as her heart directed. It just made me love them more.

And tonight, two days before the big day, we were decorating the tree. It was not a live tree, much to Jared's disappointment. It seemed our lovely nanny was allergic, and since we needed Candace more than we needed a live tree, the fake pine was now set up in the corner.

"I'm really sorry to put a crimp in your traditions," Candace said, for the umpteenth time, as we carried boxes of ornaments down from the attic.

"Don't sweat it. Honestly, I'm down with a fake tree. Less of a fire hazard, and there won't be all those dead needles to contend with."

"As if you ever vacuumed up the pine needles," Jared tossed out as he followed us down the stairs. I stuck my tongue out at him. "But he's right, Candace, it's fine. It's a fat, beautiful tree and no one will notice that it's not a real one once all the ornaments are hung."

She nodded, her long black hair braided and pinned to the back of her head, but it was obvious she didn't believe my husband.

We placed the boxes on the floor. I went to make us coffee, Jared turned on some holiday music, and Candace began nosing through the ornaments while the baby slept.

When I padded out into the living room with three cups of coffee on a tray painted with holly berries and leaves, Jared was dangling a cardboard pair of skates in the air as Candace listened. She was much shorter than Jared. A little on the plump side, with warm eyes and a loving personality. She'd quickly become indispensable to us. She also had the Jean Rowe stamp of approval so it was obvious she was magic.

"…made this when he was in kindergarten." He flipped the skates around. "His lowercase y is backwards. He had the worst times with his Ys. One time, in utter frustration as he practiced his letters he yelled at us, 'Why did you name me Ryker with a Y? I want to be a Ryker with an I!'"

"Like Will Riker?" I asked while placing the tray on the coffee table. Jared nodded. "Oh man, I am so calling him Number One the next time I see him."

That made Jared smile. He'd been kind of bummed when Ryker had called a few days ago to say he just didn't have time to do Mom and us, and since he'd been here at Thanksgiving…

"I love the homemade ornaments. My tree is covered with them as well. Pretty soon you'll have all kinds of artwork that Charlotte will bring home," Candace said as I handed her a mug.

I liked the thought of that. A lot. As carols filled the house we strung the lights and the garland, then said goodbye to Candace. She had the next few days off as we had three whole days of no hockey. The game this afternoon against Carolina was our last until December 27, which was an away game in Boston, and Charlotte was coming to the rink with us to spend time with Noah's nanny.

"I got us something," Jared spoke up as we worked away in quiet companionship while Elvis sang gospel songs in the background.

I peeked around the tree. "The UPS man has been making daily stops and you say that as if I'll be surprised."

"Not all of those boxes and bags are mine," he said as he placed the delicate gold heart that read *First Christmas Together* on a small bough right under the glowing white star.

"True, half are mine," I conceded. It was impossible to shop for gifts and play hockey and travel and tend to a baby. There was barely time for sex anymore. Once a week was a dramatic dip. Hmm, now that I thought of sex it seemed like a good time to grab a piece. Lottie was asleep. Candace had gone home. If we hurried we could—

The baby started to whimper upstairs. "I'll get her. I want to show you what came today."

I smiled, bobbed my head, and then sighed as he climbed the stairs. I made a circuit of the tree as Jared talked to our daughter upstairs. His quiet chit-chat as he changed her warmed my heart. There was one gaping hole in the front that needed something so I rummaged around in the empty box, pushing tissue paper and a few boxes of extra hooks aside.

"Okay, I have two beautiful things to share with you," Jared said as he came down the stairs, Lottie in his arms, and long silver box sticking out of his front pocket. "Here, can you take her?"

"Of course." I scooped her up and nuzzled her soft hair. She cooed and gurgled and slapped me in the ear with a tiny fist. "She's been watching Uncle Brady's old game tapes."

Jared snickered as he pulled the box from his front jean pocket. "I know it's a little extravagant, but when I saw it in the online catalogue I just…well, I just knew we had to have it."

"The way you talk it's made out of gold or something," I teased while cradling a sleepy baby.

"Not quite gold," he whispered, lifting the lid then removing a fragile-looking glass ornament. It was a pair of white, snowy baby booties with *Charlotte's First Christmas* delicately painted across the tiny boots, the date under the personalization. "It's so hard to find things that aren't pink or blue."

"It's perfect, totally amazingly perfect!" I moved closer and grabbed a kiss. He looked so pleased. "Hang it right there in the front in that space."

"That's why I left it bare there." Lottie and I watched as her dad draped the tiny hook over the short bough. Jared stepped back, crossed his arms, and tipped his head. "What do you think?"

"I think everything is perfect."

The next morning, after our daughter woke us at four for a bottle and a clean diaper, we girded ourselves for the coming invasion. A peaceful breakfast out at our favorite eatery, a trendy little bagel shop with a hundred different kinds of bagels and the best white hot chocolate on the planet. Charlotte was well-behaved and Jared and I ate our bagels in peace, not one person coming over to talk or get a selfie or an autograph. Not that I minded interacting with the fans, quite the contrary, but every so often it was nice to be out and just be left alone.

"It's time to go," Jared said after a quick glance at his phone. "The first wave will arrive at ten."

I popped the last bite of my asiago bagel into my mouth, sighed, and nodded.

"Right. Let's do this."

We gathered Lottie up, covered her with a blanket, and made our way into the cold. There was snow on the way according to the weather, but not for another day. In a way, and I knew this was really selfish of me, I had kind of hoped that the snow would have come today. That way it would've been just Jared, Charlotte, and me for Christmas.

"It'll be fine," Jared said as we pulled away from the bagel shop.

"I know, but the noise. All the noise, noise, noise, noise, noise." I made a dizzy face then crossed my eyes. At times, the din did get to me, when I had one of those rare headaches that popped up out of nowhere.

"You sound like the Grinch," Jared joked and patted my knee.

"Yeah, I guess. That may have been an overstatement."

Six hours later I knew that I'd not overstated the noise. Brady and his family were there, Jamie and his, and my parents. Oh, and Bourque of course. There was little perfection to be found, but oh man was there lots of noise. Six kids, seven if one counted Lottie, made a ton of racket. Charlotte was fussy and uneasy with all the yelling and hooting her cousins made all day long. Once evening rolled around and the kids quieted, Lottie began to settle a bit.

"Do we really have to watch *Frozen* again? Seriously, there has to be a new Disney movie to watch," Jamie moaned when we all gathered for family time. Mom was adamant about us all sitting down as a whole to see a holiday movie.

"I vote for *Die Hard*," Brady tossed out and got a grunt of disapproval from his wife. "What? It's a Christmas movie."

"We're not letting the girls watch a terrorist fall off a building," his wife quickly retaliated.

"Fine, how about *Home Alone*?" Jamie offered as he scratched Bourque's head.

"That movie is scary," one of the Brady's twins replied, I wasn't sure which one, they both looked and sounded the same.

"It's not scary, it's funny," Jamie argued but was rapidly outvoted.

"How about *Holiday Inn* with Bing Crosby?" Mom suggested as she patted Charlotte's back hoping for a burp.

"What's a Bing Crosby?" twin number two asked. Or maybe it was the same twin as before, who knows?

"I feel so old," Dad moaned from the recliner.

"Okay, I have it," I called from the floor with the kids, my back on the couch as I rested between Jared's legs. I stole the remote from Brady, who always had it because he thought he was the lord of the remote or something. Oldest brothers are the worst. I pulled up my favorites list.

"I swear to God, if you pick *Jingle all the Way* I will whip you with a sock," Brady growled as I hit play on *Jingle all the Way* then sniggered. Which got me a sock to the face as Arnold Schwarzenegger's best comedy movie *ever* started playing. A small footwear battle broke out when I flung Brady's balled-up sock at him, which ended with one of my socks hanging from the top of the star on the tree.

"Okay, boys, that's enough," Mom chided.

"Yeah, boys," Jamie teased right before the sock wad hit him in the face. He snorted eggnog up his nose on impact which, when it came out in a massive sneeze, made Brady and me roll on the floor in glee.

"You'd think when they got older they'd settle down a bit," Mom said with a classic Jean Rowe eye-roll. Jamie dabbed the eggnog off his shirt while he snorted with laughter.

When I sat down I found Charlotte staring at me in utter confusion. That made me laugh even harder. Her little eyebrows were tangled and her blue-green eyes narrow. I lifted her from my mother then sat back down between Jared's legs.

"See what kind of insanity you've been born into, Lottie Lou?" I crooned at her, and the furrows on her brow softened.

"The best kind of insanity," Jared whispered beside my ear. "The kind that a close-knit, loving family brings."

Looking around at the Rowes gathered in our house, I could only nod.

THE END

A RAILERS NOVELLA

RIVALS

RJ SCOTT &
V.L. LOCEY

A note from the authors

When we were writing this in November 2021, the NHL was intending to send players to the Beijing Olympics in February 2022. The full rosters were to be announced in December, but there were already significant concerns regarding NHL attendance at an event in a country that has many human rights issues, and of course, the COVID pandemic. Of biggest concern to us both was the treatment of LGBTQ+ people, and that informs the story we have written. We wanted to show our heroes—Ten, Tate, Stan, Jared, Ryker, Colorado, Bryan, Vlad—skating for their countries as rivals, yet have a thread of love running through everything, which is what we have done. That love is not allowed in the country where the Olympics are being held.

We didn't know at that time whether the NHL would attend and they didn't have to make their decision until the 10th of January, but they made the decision not to attend before Christmas—after we were nearly done with edits.

We both wish the NHL would have stayed away to take

a stand for human rights, but it was never likely, and as it is, COVID has done the job for them.

So, this novella is now a fantasy about NHL players attending the Olympics—we've taken poetic license with a lot of plot points and have been driven by our characters, who represent many parts of the queer spectrum. As of today, we're not even sure there will be an All-Star Weekend, but we've written in a non-COVID world, and as you might expect, Ten and Tate would both be voted in as All-Stars.

In the book, Ten writes an article, and his thoughts and comments are very much our own.

We hope you love their story.

RJ & Vicki
Xxx

Chapter One

Jared

"The name is wrong on my bag." Ten shoved his Team USA kit bag onto the bed, right on top of my neatly folded T-shirts. "I filled in the form *Madsen-Rowe* and look!" He pointed at the single word *ROWE* that appeared in several places on the bag. I gently picked it up, and placed it to one side, then smoothed out my small supply of official team shirts in all their red and white glory. Ten had been a flurry of motion today—the last few hours before attending the All-Star game, and then flying direct to Beijing—and he hadn't stopped since three this morning when he'd woken up flailing and muttering about bacon. God knows what he'd been dreaming about, but if it involved his beloved bacon, then it had to be serious.

"I'll get you a marker, and you can add the Madsen," I teased, but I hadn't read the room, because Ten slumped to the bed, only just missing my folded tees.

"I miss Charlotte already, and we're doing this huge thing, and they can't even get my name right."

Okay, this was serious, so I picked up the shirts and placed them out of harm's reach, then sat next to my fretting husband, hugging him, and resting my cheek on his hair. "I miss her as well," I murmured, then felt and heard his whole-body sigh.

"I know she'll be fine with Mom—spoiled—and I know it's only a while, but I wish she was coming with us, and I wish they'd gotten my name right. It's like they forgot I'm married." He suddenly tensed; "Holy shit, what if my jersey is wrong as well." He stood then, shook me off, and raced out of the room with a resounding, *no fucking way!*

As soon as he'd gone, I checked my official duffle, and thankfully, saw that the full name was stitched onto it.

"Something else that makes Canada better," I said smugly to no one, and then realized that I should be more upset on Ten's behalf. The fact we had been picked to represent our countries on opposing teams hadn't come between us in any way—apart from the constant teasing I got from the Rowe brothers with their stupid-ass childish "*USA is better*" chant in the family chat, which I could mostly ignore. I took the higher ground and simply sent them a picture of the Canadian team in 2014, which was my way of saying "take-that-team-USA". Funnily enough, both the Rowe boys and I ignored 2018—some things were best not spoken about, and we were all getting tired of Stan waxing lyrical about the Russians.

There was a healthy rivalry among us all, friends and family alike, but in my heart I kind of dreaded the aftereffects of losses where national pride was concerned. Canada wasn't just my birthplace, it was in my heart, and I was proud of my heritage, and being chosen as one of the Team Canada assistant coaches made me want to burst with pride, and of course I wanted to beat Team USA soundly. But as Ten's husband, I wanted him to win because I was so proud of him, and he was one of the best players of his generation, and he deserved to win. But then, Ryker was Team Canada, and to see my son win a medal would be the pinnacle of hockey-dad life.

I already had a gold medal from 2014, part of the victorious Canada team, although to be fair, I'd ridden the bench for most of it. Still, I'd played in that final game, and I'd been part of the team that had taken gold. I wanted that for Ten, but I wanted it for Ryker as well.

I was confused, and patriotic, and then more confused, and then a proud spouse, and father, and friend, and really, all I wanted to do was get to Beijing and start coaching some hockey.

The entire Railers team had ended up at our place to watch the opening ceremony. Depending on whether a player had been at the All-Star weekend, guys like Ten, Tate, and Stan, wouldn't be arriving until a full three days after the opening ceremony, but with an intense season and not a day to spare no NHL player would make the grand beginnings of the games at all. So instead, every single one of us had stared in awe at the beautiful Beijing National Indoor Stadium and cheered as our various teams behind the flags of our countries passed by. Stan cried, which not even one of us laughed at. This was overwhelmingly intense.

It was disappointing, and maybe we got a better view watching it on the TV, but still, to have been there, parading for our countries? That would have been awesome.

Ten arrived back with his cell phone to his ear; "… and that's non-negotiable!" he snapped, and then ended the call with a terse goodbye.

I winced. "Who were you shouting at?"

"Ed, our team equipment manager," he groused, and then his eyes widened. "Shit, I just shouted at poor Ed, the wonderful, *amazing*, team equipment manager."

I stayed quiet—Ten was placid off the ice, passionate about his sport, but he was never rude, and I could see all those emotions passing over his face.

"Shit," he said again, and then pressed redial, and slunk out of the bedroom, probably so I didn't hear him apologizing to Ed, who was a perfectly nice man and didn't deserve anyone being a diva. I carried on packing, knowing the bulk of what we needed would already be in Beijing with the start of the tournament only a week away. We'd practiced some, shifted lines around, but none of the teams had real ice time after the qualification rounds.

My biggest issue was with the final six D-men I was going to recommend to Abraham Devers, the Canadian head coach for the duration, who coached for New York in the season. I already had a short list of seven from the pool I'd been given, but I'd not physically played with any of them, and the notebooks I'd filled with details weren't making the picture any clearer.

I'd even taken to checking out social media to see what the fans said, but I got stuck on the *Ten!Watch* website, reading on the forum about how the sexiest player in the world was Ten, and how no defenseman from *any* country could touch him. Of course, I agreed with the sexiest part, and felt a sudden urge to kiss some of his stress away. Still, I had a few defensemen who made Ten work hard, him and Tate Collins both, and yet again, I went from angsty to proud and back again.

"Ed's forgiven me," Ten dropped his cell onto the bed and sat down so heavily I swore the frame creaked. "I told him about Charlotte, and the way that…" He stopped and scrubbed his eyes.

I tugged him in for a hug, then did this complicated flip maneuver that had him under me, his mouth slack with shock. Then, I proceeded to kiss him soundly, and after a short while, he relaxed into the mattress. We didn't have time for more, but this was enough to ground him *and* me.

His cell chimed with a familiar tone that he had for his family. We scrambled up together in panic, and he answered it immediately. The video call connected, and we were face-to-face with our beautiful daughter, who stared at the screen and then pointed at us.

"Dadda! Pappa!" she said, and then turned away, probably to talk to Ten's mom, Jean, who shuffled into view so we could see them both.

"Hey, Lottie!" Ten called, and Lottie gave the widest grin, holding up a toy bear and waggling it at us. She was over a year now, and while she was linking a few words, it was mostly sounds and waving toys. She was everything to us. She was bigger than us, bigger than hockey, and worth more than any Olympics—and that was what we needed to remember.

"We just had pancakes," Jean announced.

"You did?" Ten said, and his grin was so wide I wondered if it would ever leave his face. "Lottie? Yummy?" he asked and made smacking noises to indicate eating.

Lottie stared at us, babbling about her teddy, but she too was smiling, and that was a nice image to take with us when the call ended.

"So, what did Ed tell you?" I asked after a short pause.

Ten flushed in embarrassment. "My jerseys have Madsen-Rowe on them," Ten said and lay back against the pillows.

"So, it's just the bag that Team USA messed up on?"

He shot me a wry look, then sighed. "I overreacted."

"Yep."

He sighed some more, then we exchanged an extra kiss. We weren't even flying out to Beijing together, me stuck in one more planning session, Ten jetting out first class after appearing in the All-Star game. He was proud to have been invited to the All-Star—an event where a ton of specially invited players went up against each other in things like hardest shot, or fastest lap. It was just bad timing that it was right before the olympics.

I laced my fingers in his. "I'll miss you," I murmured, and pressed my forehead to his. We'd done everything together for so long, apart from the Stan/Elvis Christmas road trip, which I still hadn't entirely forgiven him for. The thought of not being together was unsettling.

"I'll miss you, too."

"We're lucky that at least we're going to be around

each other, Stan spent an hour in the chat talking about how Erik is staying back here."

"Was that before or after he talked about how Russia is best."

We both chuckled then because since he, Ten, and Bryan Delaney, the Railers' second goalie, had been signed up by their countries, Stan had been like a broken record.

"I need to finish packing." He rolled off the bed, and I had to restrain myself from tugging him back and pinning him down so I could get some more kisses. Instead, I settled for watching him tuck one of Lottie's tiny teddies into his bag, and then doing the same for me. Finally, we couldn't delay things any longer, and it didn't help that a team car was outside for him, and he really had to go. I stopped him at the door, grasping his hand.

"Good luck," I murmured into a kiss.

"Good luck," he whispered. Then, he lifted a single eyebrow and, with his best impersonation of Stan, growled: "USA best," then darted away before I could squash him like a bug. He waved as he got into the car, and I waved, making a heart with my hands and sighing as the car went through the gates, watching them close behind him.

Now it was just me, and my car wasn't going to arrive for a while. I couldn't join Ten at the All-Star Game, instead I was heading out to a coach's camp, so I didn't know what to do with myself. I tidied away a few of Lottie's toys, checked I had everything I needed, checked it again, locked up the house, unlocked the back door to relock it, just so I knew it was done. Anything to kill time.

Finally, I checked some game tape. Only it wasn't for

Team Canada. Nope, it was my old favorite—the first time Ten had gotten back on the ice after his accident.

I had it bad.

Which was good.

The airport was manic, but at least we didn't have the fanfare on leaving that Team USA did—boarding from New York, there were crowds of supporters. While we did have some fuss, we weren't Team USA flying out of an American city, so the players got some attention, but luckily, myself and the other coaches slipped through mostly unnoticed. That meant I got to sit and chat with our head coach, and while Abraham Devers was normally a rival on ice, this time I could talk frankly about the D-men I was working with and the three who were giving me issues. The players were at the back of the plane, us at the front, along with a couple of the figure skating coaches, and thankfully, we could use the time to talk.

"So, the three we need to discuss?"

"Jennings, Hennessey, and LaFleur," I reeled off the names easily enough, and Devers nodded. "My instinct is to keep Hennessey in reserve." At only twenty, he was the youngest of the three, and was so damn fast no one could keep up, but what we lacked in defense was the big guys, the ones who could protect our forwards—protect Ryker. Not that I was thinking that way, I was a professional, and Ryker was one of several forwards who needed protection. We had to go for bulk and brawn over speed sometimes.

"Agreed, I like what Hennessey brings to the table, and we can switch him in if needed. It's the US side we have to be careful with, Tate and Ten." He side-eyed me, and I waited for him to ask me if I had insider information, but all he did was smile. "Tate and Ten, the dream team," he added. "But we have Ryker, and he's a chip off the old block, don't you think?"

Enormous pride welled inside me, but I didn't give anything away.

"I couldn't say," I finally offered.

We bumped fists, and then Devers sat back in his seat, iPad on his chest, staring at game film. "This could be our Olympics," he mused.

I sat back as well, lovingly hugging my clipboard with the penciled in names, my bible of skills, my list of awesome, and let myself imagine for a moment Team Canada getting the gold. Then, getting a squirrely feeling in my chest at the thought of Ten not winning, and then, thinking about Ryker, again.

Fuck my life.

This could be rough.

Chapter Two

Ten

... so, while I'm thrilled to be representing my country as one of an estimated two hundred plus LGBTQ athletes attending the winter games, I'm also more than a little nervous. The country that is hosting the games has begun a crackdown on LGBTQ accounts and social media sites. I'm travelling into a foreign land that has no marriage equality and has banned "abnormal sexual behaviors" (aka homosexuality) from any sort of media. I have to wonder what that will mean to me and my fellow LGBTQ athletes. Will we be targeted for erasure from televised games? Will our queer status keep our games from being broadcast out of our host country? Will we be scorned publicly by the government who invited us when we step outside of the Olympic Village with our significant others? Sadly, this is what LGBTQ Olympians have to always keep in mind. For as many advances that we have witnessed there is still a long road to travel to find true equality. We

will continue the fight, though. Not for ourselves, but for the young athletes who will follow.

Tennant Madsen-Rowe
Team USA Men's Hockey
Harrisburg Railers

I sat back, straightening my spine as I read over the short article. I was no author—that was for sure. Miss Billings, my high school English teacher, could attest to that fact.

I glanced out at the fluffy white clouds as we soared over the ocean, rolling my shoulders, and wishing I could call my mother. Not just to check on Lottie, but to have her proofread this stupid article. I was wiped out after the All-Star Game with Tate Collins. The game itself hadn't been taxing, but the stress of all the publicity, combined with the Olympics… well, my mind was crispy. Tate and I had missed the official team flight, but weren't even on the same plane now. Just another pressure point that muddled my head. So yeah, this article was garbage, probably.

Any time I had to do this kind of thing—speak publicly or pen something for a major media outlet—I got a sour gut. Being the spokesman for queer puck-pushers had never been my goal. Truly. All I'd ever wanted was to play hockey, fall in love, get married, and have a family. Did it really matter if my spouse was male or female? Did that honestly have one *damn* thing to do with my ability to score? No. No, it did not. But there we were, a few years after I'd come out, fighting the same battle. Sometimes, it felt as if we were losing ground. Somedays, I just wanted to be Ten, the hockey player with the so-so slapshot skills.

Sadly, the world wasn't ready to let me, or any LGBTQ public figure, be a simple jock. Which sucked.

But yeah, deal with it Tennant. You knew what you were getting into. Just re-read your piece for Queer Athlete Monthly *and stop whining.*

"Would you like another soda, Mr. Madsen-Rowe?"

I smiled at the flight attendant. She was a lovely Asian woman with short black hair and clipped, but precise, English. Flying first-class on Air China was like checking into a luxury hotel. The pod-style flat bed seats were firm and spacious with a nice pillow and duvet. The meal had been excellent. The service exemplary. The movies offered in English were okay, not too many recent releases, but that was acceptable. I would probably just check out a few podcasts I'd downloaded before leaving, then see if I could get some sleep. Sixteen hours in the air was going to kick my ass big time. But hey, we didn't have to skate until tomorrow. Or was it today in China? Whatever.

I'd get time to find my room and crash. Hopefully, my roommate would be cool and not a partier. There had been quite the lengthy discussion about gay couples rooming together in the Olympic Village. I'd kind of dug my heels in, as had a few others, to say that it was total bullshit that some straight couples could sleep with their spouses, but not us. Jared and I had no male/female room rules to adhere to after all. Tons of wrangling began between governments and officials. It started to get a little ugly when Jared broke the deadlock by saying that, while he was not happy about being looked down upon for being married to me, he would, in true diplomatic style, sleep in his own room with Team Canada. He cited that it would be better in the long run, as differing schedules, as well as us officially being rivals, would make separate beds less dicey for all involved. That was what he said. I doubted he truly felt that way, but the man was a peacemaker.

While I'd been pissed at first, I came to see that sometimes you had to bend. Like a willow in the wind. Was sharing a bed the hill I wanted to die on for my first Olympics? Yes. Yes it was, but it also wasn't. Complaining bitterly, I withdrew my complaint on the condition that my husband and I be able to visit each other's rooms without censure from our teams or the governing committees. That drew some flak from a few less progressive countries, but in the end, willow in the wind, baby. They met me halfway. Well, less than halfway. It was kind of like they won and I lost for the most part, but I'd planted my fucking rainbow flag on that mountain. Fuck yeah. Go me. What we got was an *if-you-get-out-by-sunrise-you're-good* agreement between the US and Canadian head coaches.

So now we had to sneak around. Like we were kids at summer camp or something. It would have been much nicer to simply have a suite and flop into bed with my legally wedded husband. Even now, weeks later, I was grumbly about it. What else was I going to do at night when we weren't playing, if not curl up with my hubby? Which brought me back to my potential roommate. He'd better be cool.

I was seriously turning into Jared, a homebody who had no desire to be out drinking and getting laid. That was what being soppily in love and being a dad did for you. I wouldn't change it for all the hookups in the world. Although, from an old married dude's point of view there were some seriously buff guys flying into Beijing. I mean big-time hot man flesh on the slopes, as well as on skates and over at the luge.

"Yes, please and thank you," I replied in what I hoped was somewhat decent Mandarin. I'd taken a crash course before leaving. Given the way she winced, I had to assume I'd butchered my reply. Being courteous, though, she nodded and went to fetch me a cold Sprite with extra ice from the galley. After my drink arrived, I slid in my earbuds, and found a show about three lighthouse keepers who'd mysteriously disappeared without a trace from a deserted island in Scotland. Jared had gotten me hooked on these kind of mystery shows. We listened to them quite often, and had even started watching some shows at night when we weren't at the barn. I had really started getting into *Only Murders in the Building* and *Mare of East Town,* while Jared had been trying to get me into some old show called *Twin Peaks* and any BBC mystery show he could find. The man was a huge British mystery fan. Like, monstrously huge.

Yawning as the lights in the cabin dimmed, I closed my laptop, tucked it back into my carry-on bag, and nestled in for my Scottish lighthouse mystery, the whining of the engines disappearing as the podcast began. I got maybe five minutes in and crashed hard, the past month of wrangling with government officials, the pre-Olympic madness, Railers hockey, marriage, family matters outside of my home, and fatherhood checked me harder than Brady ever had. And my eldest brother had knocked me into an alternate universe several times.

When I came to, many hours later, we were about an

hour away from Beijing Capital International Airport. The jitters turned into a full-blown case of anxiety that torqued my brain into one of those miserable headaches—long-term post-concussive symptoms, in doctor talk—that would level me like a migraine. As the pressure in my head began to build I dug into my carry-on to find the sumatriptan I'd been prescribed for the post-traumatic headaches. Big thanks to Aarni "Fuckface" Lankinen for gifting me with these beauties after that slew-foot-slash-brain-bleed-cut-throat incident that had nearly ended my career.

I winced at the sounds and lights of the bustling airport. An Olympic representative met me at my gate. Chinese, smiling, happy to meet me. His name was Bingwen. His smile was infectious. Or it would have been, had I not been battling nausea.

Thank God someone had sent somebody to collect me and my luggage. I'd not have been able to manage it on my own without puking into a trash can, and wouldn't that have been a nice look for Team USA?

It looked like it was going to be a long night. Man, I hoped my roommate was the shy, retiring type.

The only thing I saw of Beijing on the ride from the airport to the hotel was the inside of my eyelids. Fingers pressed to my left wrist, I whispered to myself to breathe in, then breathe out. It was a yogic breathing technique one of my sports neurologists had recommended when I'd been to Philly to see him about the headaches last summer. It had been him who had given me the migraine meds, which helped tremendously, as well as passing along alternative and holistic ways to combat the headaches. Some had worked, some hadn't. Pressure points and yogic breathing had seemed to be a way I could pull back from the stimulation of the outside world when my head was throbbing. It eased things just enough to give the sumatriptan time to start working.

"We're here now. Mr. Madsen-Rowe," Bingwen informed me after a damn short ride. "Would you like me to call for a doctor from your team?"

"Nope, no, I'm good," I lied, slipping on some sunglasses as I forced myself to sit up in the seat. Plastering on a smile that felt like a grimace, and probably was, I somehow managed to follow my guide through the hustle and bustle in the lobby of one of several new high-rise buildings. I got checked in and stumbled along behind Bingwen into an elevator. My fingers resting on my pulse, eyes closed, I breathed all the way up to the seventh floor and was handed over to someone from Team USA. Chip... or had he said his name was Flip? No, Chip. Definitely Chip. He might be blond, so yeah, a Chip. And he had a lanyard. All Chips had lanyards. I had no clue what the lanyard said, but he sounded official, and dumped a cubic shit-ton of official team gear that I *must*—he was super emphatic about that—wear anywhere in the village. Bumping down the corridor, shoulder rubbing along newly painted walls, I tried to send Jared a message to let him know I was in Beijing.

. . .

T-Hey, landed, head is bad. Going to bed. Love you. <3

Not five seconds later my husband hit me back.

J-Wish I were there to rub your temples.

T-Yeah me too, baby.

J-Rest. Take meds. Will text you in the morning. <3 xx

"Okay, here we go. You're in room 8011 with a roommate. You have your team schedule, so refer to that to know where to go. Downstairs are lounges, entertainment areas, and several restaurants for the athletes. Please, always be aware that you are representing Team USA and act accordingly. Good luck."

Flip Chip handed me a key card and ran off. Squinting at him through my sunglasses, I had to wonder if he was the only rep to meet and greet every American athlete. If so, Flip Chip was going to be fried by this time tomorrow. While using the doorframe to hold me up, I scanned my card, groaned at the *beep*, and pushed into the room. It was dark, but oh fuck, was it loud.

I dropped my armful of team gear—shirts, shorts, socks, hats, flags, and who knew what else—hit the floor as I threw my hands up to cover my ears. Even with my hands blocking the sound, Aerosmith's "Walk This Way" filled my head, the screaming lead guitar making my eyes water.

"*Dude!*" I bellowed, the throbbing inside my skull steady as my own pulse now.

The bathroom door flew open, steam rolling out, and my bleary eyes took in a tall, sinewy goalie, his shoulder-length dark hair plastered to his head, tattoos covering his arms, chest, and part of his throat. He jogged out to embrace me in nothing more than some wild paisley print robe that hung open to reveal his substantial dick.

"Tennant, my man, I am *so* glad you're here! This place is pretty cool, right? I mean, you should check out the acoustics in the bathroom. Enormously righteous reverb. I'm stoked that I brought my guitars! Are you loving the soundtrack?! Sure, you do. I mean, who doesn't fucking worship Steven Tyler? Totally right. Hey, are you okay, bro? You look kind of—oh *fuck*, dude!"

I threw up all over Colorado Penn.

That'll teach him not to cover his junk.

Chapter Three

Jared

I sent a final heart to Ten, just as my roommate, fellow Canadian and goalie coach, Oliver Lake, stepped into the room and collapsed boneless on the bed—the snacks he'd gone out to find tumbling from his hands. Oli had just slipped out to the machine in the corridor, which was full of healthy stuff that made me wince. I wasn't sure I was going to manage my time here without chocolate of some sort. Only, slipping out had taken him nearly an hour, but I'd just imagined him caught up with something important and ignored my rumbling belly.

"No more," he muttered.

I liked Oli, although I didn't know him too well, given he was coaching for Vegas, who we only met a couple of times a year. Still, he was friends with our goalie coach, knew Stan, and had been to a couple of Railers' events. Married to Elsa, with three kids, he was a family man who had already asked to see photos of Lottie, then showed me his three.

"No more what?" I asked from my bed, with my tablet on my knees. "Did you get caught by someone?"

"Not someone. *All* the people," he groaned and covered his eyes. "Don't go out there," he added, "it's not safe." He tossed me a granola bar, which I caught deftly and placed next to me. "Worst of all, no chocolate anywhere." A ton of staff and skaters had descended over the course of today, and I knew that we had the entire Team Canada hockey team here, because I'd made a point of ticking everyone off the list. It was something I did to take my mind off the fact I was missing Lottie and Ten. To the point where I was close to slinking over to the Team USA building just to reassure myself Ten was there and okay.

My poor husband said he had a headache, and knowing his ability to make light of the levels of pain he was in, I bet it was a doozy. I hoped he didn't get sick, because normally I'd be there to hold him quietly until the meds kicked in and he felt better. I guessed whomever he was rooming with was responsible for that now, and I hoped to God it was someone quiet and respectful, who knew he needed downtime.

I opened the wrapper of my energy bar and took a bite of the dry oaty not-goodness, staring at my screen and wondering what I wasn't seeing when I looked at my seven potential D-men choices. They were all good on paper, their stats clean, three of them were big bruiser-type guys, the other four were fast on their skates, and all of them were my first choices when it came to offering names for the team.

"Why is this so hard?" I huffed.

Oli rolled onto his side to face me. "What?"

"Seven D-men, six places to start."

"Tell me about them."

There are more than a few things different about playing in the Olympics—from the size of the rink to the incredible pressure to be "on" every second we were outside our rooms. The rinks here were fifteen feet wider than a typical NHL-er was used to, and on paper it gave an advantage to anyone who played in Europe, given they already used the Olympic-size rinks. None of the three remaining players I had on my list had played in Europe, but they'd managed to cover the remainder of the ice—still the larger space favored the forwards, and stretched the D-men, particularly in the standard three-on-two situation.

"Jennings, Hennessey, and LaFleur are the three I'm struggling with, I've seen all of them up against Ten and Tate, and Hennessey is strong, but he never comes off as confident when he's faced with those two."

"We don't meet the US until after China and Germany," he reminded me.

I knew that, but it was the US that was giving me hives, for many reasons. I didn't want to say I wasn't worried about China, because that would be naive—one wrong bounce, one unlucky day, and losing to China could be the biggest humiliation for Canada with its heritage and its medals. I mean, we finished in the bronze position four years ago, and the nation mourned. Germany on the other hand, was a strong team, but we'd played against a lot of the key players in Railers' games, and I knew we could beat them.

On a good day.

Please let Team Canada have all the good days, and no bad days at all.

"Games against China and Germany to start pool play should help us gain confidence before our first real test against the US, but with their team and the way it's shaping up, it *would* be a test."

"Yep, Colorado is in net, and he's a crazy son of a bitch, but so good."

I had a sudden awful thought that Ten would be rooming with the mad-as-a-bunch-of-frogs-hard-rock-loving goalie, but no one on Team USA would be that cruel. Right?

"We want to earn that fourth seed and a bye into the quarterfinals." I pushed aside all my worries about Ten long enough to tap my screen and pull up the stats I needed.

I will not worry about Ten. I will not worry about Ryker.

"Yep, that bye would be good." Oli moved, then, to sit on the side of his bed, and I copied his position. Most of what was decided on game day would start with the small discussions between coaches and players back in their rooms—off-the-record comments forming the groundwork for discussions on ice. We'd be getting practice in tomorrow, the first time our guys could put aside their differences and work as a team in a while.

"We have Di Costa in goal, he likes LaFleur's style,

said he hopes that LaFleur gets a start as one of the Ds in front of him."

I made a note of that. Chemistry on ice was a thing. Take Ten and Tate for example—yes they were stars, but they had history playing for Dallas when Tate had overshadowed Ten, and I wasn't stupid enough to have taken note of there being potential problems between them. It felt disloyal, and yet again, I felt that pinch of worry over whether I should have accepted this coaching offer for my country's team. Ten and Tate would both be on the powerplay, no doubt there, and that was when the quality of the defensemen we ran in front of the goalie came into effect.

"Noted," I said, and glanced over at him, waiting for more.

"If I can get your feedback on Delaney, then do you want my opinion on the other two?"

"Always. And as for Bryan? He's a good goalie, solid, works well with Stan, knows some of Stan's moves. Doesn't choke in the big games, a good choice." I loved Bryan, from our connection to the Railers, to the more serious link between Ten, him, and Aarni *freaking* Lankinen. Bryan was quiet, but he had hawk eyes and could pull off the most impossible moves—he was a good addition to the Canadian team and deserved to be here.

Oli smiled. "For what it's worth, I would keep Hennessey in reserve."

"That was my thought as well." I felt almost vindicated that my opinion was shared by someone else—being a coach is isolating at the best of times.

"Oh, I meant to say that I saw Ryker outside." Oli gestured to the door. "Turns out he's sharing with Sawyer."

Joe Sawyer, Vancouver, was a young player with hockey smarts—well, younger than Ryker at least—he was a nice guy and had been to a couple of barbecues back home.

I wonder if Ryker misses Jacob with the same soul-wrenching tear that I miss Ten? I wonder if Ten is okay? I hope Ten doesn't need me. I need Ten. Shit! I really need to keep my head in the game here. Oli was still talking.

"Didn't get to chat to him though. He seemed real pissed about something, but he looks good in the red and white."

Pride flooded me. My son was going to be out there, playing for his country. And my husband. *And oh, shit, here I go again.*

I scrubbed at my eyes, and Oli chuckled.

"Guessing you're thinking about Ryker going up against Ten?"

"No! Yes." Then I added sheepishly: "Maybe."

"Must be hard."

"It's not easy," I conceded. Then it hit me that he said Ryker was pissed. "What was messing with Ryker?"

"He didn't say, muttered some shit about Finland, which he should probably keep to himself." I put the tablet down and rolled my neck.

"I might go track him down, maybe he needs his—"

"Dad?"

"I was going to say assistant coach, asshole."

"You know he's a forward, right?"

"Whatever." I grabbed another oat bar, shoved it into

my pocket, and shrugged on my official Team Canada jacket, the weight of it all in my mind, but filled with the responsibilities of an entire country. I headed down the one flight of stairs that took me to one of many athletes' floors, where hockey players, figure skaters, and a couple of snowboarders rubbed shoulders. There was a large open room at one end, with the snack dispenser, and a table of mugs and drink options. I poked my head in, looking for a familiar head of curly hair.

"Coach!" one of the team called, and I recognized Sawyer, the kid sharing with Ryker. "If you're looking for…" He paused and seemed to think twice about shouting across the room, jogging over to me, trying not to spill his energy drink. "If you're looking for Ry, he's in with Delaney. Room 1421."

"Thanks." I waved at the others in the room, recognizing most of my D-men, and turned before I could get asked any leading questions about who was starting where.

1421 was right down at the other end of the corridor, and I got waylaid three separate times. It took me an entire fifteen minutes to get to the room. Oli was right—there were too many people here right now, and the excitement was overwhelming, despite how tired everyone looked. I finally reached the door and knocked on it softly—just in case Ryker wasn't in there and Bryan had decided on an early night. He was a quiet guy, and I imagined he'd be the kind to get on with sleep, but then again, who knew with goalies?

Ryker opened the door, and when he saw it was me, he gestured me in and shut us inside. I pulled him in for a quick hug that reassured me he was there, and then stepped back.

"Oli sent me down," I lied, because I really didn't want to come over as the coach who tracked down his son at every given moment. "Said you were vocal about…"

I stopped talking when I glanced over at Bryan and saw him with his back to us, a helmet next to him on the bed, talking on the phone. Ryker pressed a finger to his lips and offered me a seat, handing me a bottle of water, and then sitting on the other bed. I didn't know who Bryan was sharing with, but there was no sign of them in person —just their bags and a Stephen King paperback on the bedside table. I frowned at Ryker, but he shook his head, and we waited for Bryan to finish his call.

"… Okay. Yeah… I can do that. I'm okay… Gatlin, I promise I'm okay… I love you too… yeah, Ryker…"—he looked back over his shoulder at us—"and Coach Madsen-Rowe… no… no I'm not doing that, I don't need to. I have Ryker, and Ten is in the next building. Stan is no more than ten minutes over, okay… yes, I will. I love you so much… bye."

I waited for someone to say something, but all I got was Bryan standing tall and lifting his chin as Ryker handed me a tablet with the Finnish roster. I read the list, familiar names leaped out at me, and then, there, right at the bottom of the freaking Finnish roster—Ten's nemesis, Bryan's abuser—Aarni Lankinen.

"No fucking way," I snapped.

Bryan nodded sadly, and Ryker sighed.

I couldn't keep my reaction inside. "Not on my watch. No."

Chapter Four

Ten

I woke the following morning feeling as if I'd been dragged through a sewer by my feet, face down in the muck, forehead bouncing off the slimy troughs filled with sludge.

Which was a typical morning after a massive headache. Add in jet lag, and yeah, I was shit-faced and not in that fun been-partying-all-night-with-my-bros kind of way.

The room was dark, thank all the gods. The only sound was of someone nearby humming and strumming on an acoustic guitar. Sitting up was done in increments. There was a slight wave of nausea and a little dizziness, also typical of a postdrome. The plucking and soft singing stopped at my groan. Inhaling deeply to counter the stomach lurch, I breathed in lavender. It was… nice.

"Morning," Colorado whispered from a vague point by

the windows. In the corner. Maybe on the floor? Fuck. This was so not what I needed today. The aftereffects of a crashing headache usually lingered for a full day after the migraine itself, and left me feeling exhausted and mentally fogged. Just the place I wanted my head to be on the day of my arrival. Go me. Ugh. "I had some ginger tea sent up. My grandmother swears by it for any kind of headaches. Also, she said to rub some lavender into your pulse points, so I kind of did that when you were sleeping. Nothing beyond your wrists though, my dude."

"Oh, uhm…" I lifted my left wrist to my nose. Yep, the smell of lavender wafted from my skin. "Thanks."

"Totally my pleasure."

Moving like a geriatric patient, I eased my bare feet to the floor. Had I undressed before crawling under the covers yesterday?

"In case you're wondering, I took off your shoes and socks, great sneakers by the way, and tucked you in."

I blinked into the darkness, the memories of yesterday slowing arriving. "I threw up on you. Oh shit, Colorado, I am so sorry."

He chuckled, then rose, his lanky frame barely visible through the room-darkening drapes. It was obvious the sun was up. "No worries. Not the first time someone has tossed chunks on me. There was that time my drummer heaved on my head on a tour bus; and then, there was that time I was in bed with a couple of twins and the one had eaten bad sushi before the show. Talk about a rancid mess. Although the shower clean-up afterwards was pretty righteous." I sat there staring at his shadowy form as he neared. *Please let him have pants on.* "You cool with some soft light?"

"We can try it," I replied gruffly.

He sat beside me, rubbed my back, and then turned on one of two wall lights between our beds. Oh hey, double beds. Nice. I winced at the glow for a moment, but the pain wasn't terrible. I'd need some Advil throughout the day, and light food, but yeah, it was going to be okay. Not great, but okay. I glanced over. Thankfully, he did have jeans on. That was it. Shredded jeans and a dangling necklace made from small green beads.

"Man, you look like Keith Richards after a bender," Colorado informed me.

I snorted and it hurt. "Ow, thanks, C." I reached up to rub the tender spot between my eyes as he began pouring me some tea from a carafe sitting on a skinny oaken stand between the beds. There was a landline phone on the table, several bracelets, and a sock that was bright pink and had koalas on it. Just one sock. Where the other one was, I had no clue. It would've required too much mental power to glance around the room.

"Here, sip on this tea. Totally natural, so don't worry." I eyed the Styrofoam cup warily. "Dude, I would not let you sip, if it wasn't totally clean."

"You didn't slip any CBD oil into it or anything?" I asked, gently taking the steaming cup from his hand. He gave me a look. "Sorry, I know you don't do dope. I shouldn't have said that. Blame it on my head."

"You're cool. Everyone assumes I'm a doper or something. Rock star goalie. The dude must be toking up nightly. But I'm as sparkling clean as your mother's bathroom sink. I don't do drugs or drink. Family reasons." He twisted around on the bed, folding his long legs into a lotus. Bendy goalies astounded me. "So, now that you're back in the land of the living, you need to know that I turned off your phone. It was pinging steadily, and you were out of it. You need to get in touch with Jared. There's some shit going down that you need to be on top of."

"Bad shit?" I asked, taking a sip of the tea, and sighing in pleasure. It was grassy-tasting with some sort of citrus undercurrents. It slid smoothly down my throat to my unruly stomach.

"Not good shit," he said, reaching around the carafe, and plucking my cell from the table where it had been plugged in all night. He unplugged it and passed it over, sharp eyes peering at me from under the soft, long strands hanging in his eyes. "I'm going to go soak my feet in what's left of the ginger tea. My big toe is inflamed from banging it on the dresser in that backpedal to avoid puke on my balls."

My cheeks flamed. "I'm *really* sorry about that."

He waved it off. "Again, no worries. Madeline tossed her cookies—like literally it was cookies and apple juice— in my lap just last week."

Okay, yeah, I'd been there myself. Nothing said being a dad like being coated with regurgitated sour milk.

"You touch base with your old man. He's probably ready to breach enemy lines to hear your voice."

"Thanks, yeah, I'll get in touch with Jared." I powered up my phone as he limped off to the bathroom. As soon as the phone was on, the flurry of incoming texts, messages, and notifications arrived in a tsunami of different tones and pings. Shit. What the hell had happened? Ignoring all the other BS, like team chats and family chats, I read through the twenty or so texts from my husband. There was nothing specific, which was doubly upsetting.

J-I know you're recovering, but we need to talk. In person. Reach out when awake.

Taking another steadying sip of tea, I fired off a text to Jared.

T-Awake now. Rough as shit, but no more than usual. What's going on?

His reply came in within seconds.

J-Hey babe, take some Advil before you do anything. Meet me at the players' lounge, ground floor, in thirty minutes.

J-Don't read the team chats. Talk to me first.

. . .

Cool. That wasn't adding any anxiety to the moment.

Rubbing at my eyes, which were a little blurry, I lifted my gaze from my phone to the bathroom door. Colorado was in there, splashing around, soaking his toe as he sang disjointed lyrics about a bruised pinkie toe named Joe. Joe the pinkie toe. It was so stupid that it made me snigger like a moron. Which felt totally out of place emotionally, given the past twenty-four hours. The silly fit made my head hurt though, so I stopped sniggering and rose from the bed, a bit shaky, but otherwise okay, and dug into my personal bag for some Advil and my shades. I was, for sure, going to need both today.

I silenced the incoming messages and weeble-wobbled my way to the bathroom door, then I politely ejected the goalie and his sore toe. There was no way I could face the world without a shower and good tooth-brushing.

Exiting the elevator, I had to have looked like some wannabe Colorado Penn.

A patriotic as fuck wannabe Colorado Penn.

With my Team USA ballcap riding on my eyebrows, wearing shades, and a red, white, and blue team jacket, I felt beyond stupid. That was until I saw my husband in a startlingly bright red and white Team Canada jacket. He walked up to me, hugged me briefly, then pulled back to stare at me.

"You look pale," he said, easing his hand to my lower back, then remembering where we were and letting his hand fall to his side. We'd all promised to be good gays and not slobber all over each other in public. Jared and I never had slippery wet PDAs anyway. He wasn't the kind of man to carry on like that in public even when he had been married to a woman.

"Colorado said I look like Keith Richards."

He winced. "Ouch."

I shrugged. "It's not a lie." I waved at a few of the other hockey players I knew. Most of them lifted a hand in return, but a few were giving me worried looks. "What's going on?" I asked and was led out of the packed lounge to the painfully bright outdoors. "Shit," I moaned, giving serious thought to going back inside.

"I looked up a place if you think you can walk a mile?"

"Yeah, I think I can do a mile." I wanted to kiss him on the mouth for all his concern. Instead, I gave him a weak smile.

"Come on." Jared steered me through throngs of athletes of every shape, size, gender, color, and nationality. I heard languages I'd never heard before. Staring up at the new high rises, I wished I'd not been so out of it on the ride from the airport. I made a mental note to see as much of this amazing city as I could before we left. Hopefully, with a gold medal. "The place I found has a rich variety of seafoods. You should take in some salmon to counter the lingering headache. Oh, and nibble on this while we walk."

He passed over a Hershey's dark chocolate bar.

"I love you," I told him as we passed a large group of Russian athletes, mostly women, who were wearing their ROC jackets and chatting away. I had to wonder if Stan was here yet. "So, talk to me." I unwrapped the candy bar, then broke off a chunk and popped it into my mouth. "What's so bad that I can't talk to my teammates?"

Jared drew in a long breath before steering me by the elbow to a long bench situated under a couple of newly planted trees. The grass looked and smelled new as well. The air was cool, not bitter cold, maybe low forties, and the sky was a gorgeous blue. I sat down gingerly. Jared settled beside me, his handsome face a mask of concern.

"We've just been notified of an emergency replacement on the Finnish team," he explained, tension lines deep around his eyes. I swallowed my candy and tossed another square into my mouth. A light wind blew across us. I motioned for him to continue. "Seems that Vilho Korkohen came down with some sort of thrush at the last minute, so the team is substituting Korkohen with Aarni Lankinen."

"Oh," I whispered, the chocolate melting on my tongue as I digested the news. "How can he be here? What about a visa, his criminal record?"

"I already checked that—he doesn't have a criminal record. I don't want you to worry though. I've already sent a protest letter to the Olympic Committee asking for them to set up a meeting with you and me, and Bryan, so that we can explain why we want Lankinen to be barred from playing for—"

"No, don't do that." I swallowed, feeling the chocolate coating my throat. Jared gaped at me. "It's okay."

"No, Tennant, it is not okay. That man—"

"We know what he did. Bryan and I… we know what he did. Let us handle it." I snapped off another square of candy and ate it as Jared sat there, wind ruffling his short blond hair, staring at me as if I had a mariachi band made up of happy salamanders playing "Las Mañanitas" on my head. "I want to face him on the ice."

"Tennant, I'm not sure that's a good idea."

"You're talking like my husband and not my coach."

"I'm not your coach! And damn right I'm talking like your husband. As the man who loves you beyond fucking reason, the thought of that slimy bastard Lankinen getting near you again makes me ragey."

"'Ragey.' Nice. You're starting to talk like me. Next you'll be listening to Marianas Trench and playing *Pokémon Quest*."

"I'm not kidding, Ten. Aarni is not someone to trifle with."

I took his hand in mine, my fingers smearing some melted chocolate over his. "I'm not trifling. I'm facing down the fucker who did this to me." I tapped my temple with my half-eaten candy bar. "He's going to be humiliated on the ice by Bryan and me. That's how we handle this."

"What if he hurts you again?"

The pain and worry in his voice broke my heart. I scooted closer, rested my head on his shoulder, and closed my eyes.

"Then you'll be there at my side like you were before." I heard him sigh as if the weight of the world were on his shoulders instead of my wonky head.

"I understand. I hate it, but I understand. I'll cancel my request for a meeting then."

I peeked up, around the bill of my hat and over the top of my sunglasses. His gaze met mine.

"I love you," I whispered.

"I love you too."

I fed him a bite of chocolate. He kissed the tips of my fingers as I pressed the sweet square between his lips, and we sat there, silently, until the candy bar was gone, my head on his shoulder. To hell with anyone who didn't like it. And to hell with Aarni Lankinen. He was about to pay the piper.

Chapter Five

Jared

It was a very different animal creating a team from the best of the best, dealing with egos, experience, and the disparate personalities that went into making up a pro athlete. It didn't matter that we were all there to play for our country; there was a ton of history between some of these guys. Take LaFleur and Smith for example, currently in a stare-off after chirping escalated from friendly banter to accusation in the space of a minute. It quickly died a death because they were professionals, but it sent ripples through the team that the coaches needed to deal with before it got out of hand.

LaFleur was a hardnosed defenseman, and one of mine to keep an eye on. After twelve years with Calgary, he had a reputation as a take-no-prisoners tough guy. Smith, on the other hand, was deadly fast—a forward Ottawa had snatched in the draft three years ago, and who proved that, sometimes speed did win over a good defense. Smith was sneaky, LaFleur was a brick wall, and their rivalry clashes in-season were legendary.

One comment about tomatoes, of all things, had started this off. The two of them were in an epic showdown like tom cats protecting their territory, complete with staring, arched backs, and hissing. Well, I might have imagined those last parts, but I bet I wasn't far off. There were protocols in place for this kind of thing, corralling the talent and cutting off any issues, and at least it wasn't a D-pair that wouldn't work together, or a center with one of his wings, but still, this wasn't the time or place for this shit.

I skated between them, herding LaFleur off to the side, grabbing an energy drink and thrusting it in his face. He was mumbling in French, but I knew more than enough French to understand that he was going to ice Smith's pretty little kisser. That sounded less like antagonism and more like unresolved sexual tension, and there was no way we could have that right now.

I went the hard-assed route. "You're on the power play with him—you think you can keep it in your pants long enough to play the freaking game?"

He stared at me open-mouthed, and then his gaze slid to Smith who'd been pulled away by Ryker. My boy was getting better at calming situations on the ice, and I didn't know where he got that from. Probably his mom, because I'd been the hot-headed one when I'd played.

"I didn't... I wasn't... I..." LaFleur tipped his chin, and any sign of shock disappeared in an instant, and back came the familiar confidence he was renowned for—with a side helping of belligerence. "Yes, Coach," he said with a smirk. God, I wanted to make him do bag skates so bad right now.

"Eyes on the prize, okay? You fuck this up, and it's on you, and you bet I will make that very clear to anyone who asks me."

He winced, and then nodded more respectfully. "Yes, Coach."

Then, he glanced over at Smith again, and this time there wasn't shock, but I didn't even want to know what was going on there, and I stared pointedly from LaFleur to Smith. Clearly, Ryker was having a similar chat with Smith, and the two combatants with their staring shit met in the middle of the ice and exchanged a cursory fist bump before skating off in opposite directions. I'd take that as a win and try to forget whatever else was happening.

The rest of the practice was mundane, with Coach calling for some line changes, working the forwards with Bryan and our other goalie, Di Costa—another twelve-year veteran who'd carried Team Canada on his back many times. I watched my skaters work drills, made a few adjustments—LaFleur tended to add theatrics, Hennessey wasn't listening—but nothing too intense, just enough to see those minute things that made me feel I was right about pairing recommendations. A commotion at the side of the rink had me glancing that way, and then doing a double take at the sea of white and blue that was the Finnish team. I knew they had the ice after us, but standing there waiting as we headed for the exit was a kick to the balls.

Some of our team crossed to them—teammates, friends

—that was the way of the NHL and its tight-knit family. Aarni stood to one side, not exactly interacting with anyone, his arms crossed over his chest, staring at something beyond us. I corralled some loose pucks that took me close to where they waited—the *away* bench— and I skated to a stop in front of Aarni. The desire to corner him and beat him to a pulp was never far away because I was the one who saw Ten's bad days, when he got a migraine or couldn't sleep. I was his husband, and I hadn't been able to protect him from Aarni, and that was the worst of everything. He'd served his suspension, pleaded out over a car accident that had nearly blinded this kid Henry, yet somehow, he was here representing his country on the greatest stage on earth.

Aarni wouldn't meet my gaze, but I think everyone went silent and knew I was staring at him. At least, all I could hear was a buzzing around me, and the familiar pull of anger and terror that seeing this asshole caused in me. I wanted to hurt him as bad as he'd hurt Ten, I wanted to corner him and—

"Coach Madsen-Rowe?" someone said next to me. I recognized the voice and glanced left to find Ryker beside me. "Dad?" he whispered in a softer tone, glancing from me to Aarni. The buzzing subsided, the terror and pain shifted a little, and I threw my wonderful son a smile.

"It's all good, Ry." I nodded, and then tapped my stick on his calf. "It's staying on the ice." Ryker skated back and away from me, and I followed him, getting caught by Coach Devers as I left the ice.

"Coach Madsen?" Coach Devers was right there next to me, and I forced every bad thought away.

"Madsen-Rowe," I corrected on instinct, and then flushed, "Sorry, I—"

"Quite right to correct me," Coach Devers said with a grimace. "I apologize and wanted to say I think you're right about Hennessey."

"That he's our backup," I said as if I hadn't missed a single beat. "We should keep him fresh for—"

"Agreed."

We stood in silence for a moment, and then Coach Devers patted me on the arm. He was one of the good guys, and someone I'd like to work with one day, if he ever came to a team where Ten was, of course.

"I need your opinion on something." He tugged me to one side. "If we get to face Finland, if Lankinen is coming at Bryan and trying to intimidate—"

"You don't need to worry. Bryan is stronger than you think, focused. He won't lose control any more than Di Costa would."

"And Ryker?"

That was a gray area. After all, Ryker and Ten were as close as brothers, even if Ten was his kind-of stepfather, and Ryker had seen for himself the aftermath of what had happened with Ten.

"We've got this," I reassured him. "The probability of meeting Finland at all is low."

"But there's always the chance that it will happen..." He raised a single eyebrow.

Finland was in group C, whereas Teams Canada and USA were group A—not even Stan with Russia in B would meet Finland straight away—but if we didn't automatically win our place through to the quarter finals, then we could be playing off against them. What if they reached the finals?

"We'll cross those bridges when we come to them," I stated.

"I can make that formal complaint—"

"No!" I winced as I cut him dead. "Sorry, no. Actually, Ten, Bryan, and Ryker want to deal with this on the ice— they need to face him down, and I respect that."

Coach Devers nodded, and we headed out of the rink to the locker room, ready to talk to the team. I shelved my hatred of Aarni, alongside my despair and temper, knowing that all three needed to be kept locked away.

I lasted exactly one more night before I headed over to Team USA in their red, white, and blue glory—feeling conspicuous in my red and white, but goddamned proud of the maple leaf on my chest. I'd hoped to subtly make my way past the security desk by flashing my pre-approved credentials, sneaking up to the fourth floor, finding Ten's room, getting a hug that I really needed, and then sneaking back out again.

Which went well until I stepped through the door. First, security had an issue, which meant I was standing by the front desk in my Canada gear, in a sea of Team USA uniforms, standing out like a *hoser* in first class.

"Jared! My man!"

I cringed because I'd just been handed back my pass, and the last person—the *very last person*—I wanted to see was Colorado Penn. The loud, and very in-your-face, rockstar goalie was about as subtle as a sledgehammer, and any hope I had of sneaking in was gone. Everyone seemed to notice I was standing there, or was that just me projecting? Colorado hug-dragged me down the corridor to the stairs.

"Don't use the elevators, dude," he announced with a sad face, "The entire speed skating team got stuck in there two hours back, and they only just got out."

"Good to know."

He slapped me on the back. "How you doing?" he bellowed, and I had my first real look at him, and had to take a second glance. Gone were the piercings, his hair was tied back, he was dressed in official USA colors, and he was not the Colorado I'd been expecting. "Yeah," he said sadly, catching my gaze, "I had to go legit even when I'm off duty, and I'm pissed, because I was rocking this new shirt with Krick on it, and the guys all had money on me taking it to the game and then… hell, you don't want to hear that, you want sexy times with your man, right?"

I glanced left and right to see if anyone heard, or cared, but we were alone by the stairs, and I thanked the heavens for that small mercy.

"To see Ten, yeah," I murmured, and began to edge away from Colorado, only he caught me, bear-hugged me as if it was perfectly normal, and then set me away.

"You've got an hour before you get noticed," he stated in all seriousness, and then sauntered off, adding a shimmy as he turned the corner.

I took the stairs to the fourth floor as fast as I could, breathless by the time I reached Ten's room, and knocking in desperation so he would open the door and I could get in before any more goalies accosted me with their weird-ass ways. Thankfully, he opened it almost immediately with a shocked expression that soon turned to pleasure.

"Jared!" he exclaimed and pulled me inside, shutting the door behind me, then hugging me as if we'd been apart a year, as if he wanted every piece of me as close to him as possible.

Or was that just me hugging him.

"I've missed you," I murmured into his neck, holding him, never wanting to leave his side again, which was just freaking stupid. I should be able to stand a few nights away… right?

He kissed me then, deeply, pushing me back against the door and cradling my face. He tasted of mint and coffee and Ten, and I couldn't get enough of him, gripping handfuls of his T-shirt and holding him tight.

"I've missed you back," Ten admitted, and slotted himself so we were hard together. I couldn't bear this touch without seeing it through. I needed so much to be closer to him, to feel his skin, to push all my worries and fears aside, and focus on us. I hated the Olympics. I hated that we were apart. I hated it all.

Actually, I loved the Olympics part, but that was something I just admitted when I was on my own.

"Is your roommate—"

"He went for coffee and to check in with Joseph and Maddie."

Joseph and Maddie? I eased away from the newest kiss when I finally put everything together, underscored by catching sight of an obnoxiously loud scarlet and orange tee lying on the second bed, complete with cartoon emu on the front. *You've got to be kidding me.*

"The fuck? Is Colorado your roommate?" Was that what he meant about the hour?

"Didn't I tell you that?" Ten appeared confused, and then brightened. "Maybe I was too messed up by the flight and resulting barfing to tell you that yes, the loudest weirdest goalie is my roommate."

"Shit, that's the last thing you need." I immediately had a long list of things that meant I was worried about the two of them sharing.

"No, he's been good, calm, sings me songs and makes me tea."

"What kind of tea?" I was suspicious because this was Colorado, and he was a rock guy, and my head was whirling with the what-ifs.

"We've got him all wrong, nothing bad at all. In fact, he's the perfect guy to share with. Well, apart from waking up to find his junk in my face."

"The fuck?" I was incensed, but Ten chuckled and kissed me again.

"It's a Colorado thing—it's all good."

I wasn't mollified at first, but when Ten went to his knees and sucked my brains out through my cock, and I returned the gift, then spent ages just kissing him and hugging him, I was okay. A discreet knock on the door had us separating and tidying up, and Ten peered through the peephole, before opening the door to Colorado, who held two stuffed emus and sported an amused smile.

"I said one hour. I gave you two. We all good?"

I kissed Ten goodbye, but couldn't resist cornering

Colorado and poking the *S* of his USA. "Keep your junk out of Ten's face," I warned him.

"Jared!" Ten huffed a laugh.

"Dude," Colorado defended at the very same time.

And then the three of us grinned at each other because the Olympics? That was some crazy shit.

Chapter Six

Ten

We were all gathered in the US team's lounge watching Russia play Switzerland.

Tate sat beside me taking notes. Honestly, that was *so* Tate Collins. Our coaches were sitting in a little cave somewhere, sequestered, watching the same game, I was sure. We'd had a light skate this morning, mostly working out any kinks and personality issues. Hockey players may be all humble in front of a camera, and for the most part that was true off camera as well, but we still had pride. Some more than others. Some so much that things got testy when one guy felt he had less of the spotlight than another.

"Fucking Stan," Tate whispered, his pencil stalling. I nodded. Yeah. Stan. If we had to face ROC later down the line, Stan was going to be a problem. He was a veteran goalie, unflappable, highly skilled, and was brick-walling it all over Switzerland. Add Vlad Novikov aka the Iceberg and Ruslan Lebedov, the captain and first line left-winger from Washington, who was leading the league in goals this year, and we would have our hands full. "You think our goalie can compare?"

We both shot looks at Colorado sitting on the floor surrounded by pillows and about ten of our teammates. I'd never seen a person with such charisma. There was something about Colorado that just drew people in, like a deity or a cult leader. Good thing he was into composing songs and blocking shots instead of anything unscrupulous. Colorado and his worshippers could take over the world. He was playing his guitar, his hair in his eyes, the soft sounds of his song barely heard over the TVs showing several different events at once.

"He's solid," I said, and found that I meant it. At first, I'd been skeptical when Colorado had been announced as part of the team. Not that he wasn't a great goalie. He was. He just lacked experience in this sort of competition. According to what he'd told me, he'd never really been *into* competitions per se, so he'd just kind of skipped them to pursue other interests. "What he lacks in experience, he makes up for with speed and that weird-ass goalie mindset."

"Hmm, yeah, I suppose. I just think there were better choices. Older netminders with more drive to excel and less drive to be a busker."

I turned my head to glare at Tate. "Dude, really? That's harsh. Coach Jamieson knows his shit. If he picked Colorado, then there was a reason."

"Yeah, I know, I just… yeah." We glanced up to see

Lebedov laser in another goal. "If we face them, we have got to keep that bastard out of his office."

I nodded. You did not let Lebedov just stand there in the left circle unchallenged for that long. The bastard was a sniper, and his one-timers were insanely hard to stop. Ask any goalie in the league, and that includes Stan. Over forty-four percent of Lebedov's goals were from his office. We wouldn't even get into his power play tallies from the circle. The man was a master of the craft. It was like watching Kareem Abdul-Jabbar's skyhook or Tom Brady rifling a pass. Things of beauty that only the elite could pull off consistently.

"We'll have to worry about Russia when we get there. Right now, we have the Chinese team to play tomorrow." I caught a bag of M&M's flying through the air towards my head. Carter Long, one of our D-men, who played under Coach Jamieson in New York, had entered the lounge with a basket of tiny bags of candy. Tate got a Snickers bar. We dove in, the small taste of home appreciated. Carter flopped down on my left, his bearded jaw working steadily as he ate his Butterfinger, his brown gaze on the ROC vs Finland game.

"They need to evict Lebedov from that circle," Carter said around his chewy mouthful.

"We were just discussing that," Tate chimed in, balling up his candy wrapper, then lobbing it at the singer and his groupies over in the corner. "Hey, music fans, think you want to pay attention to the competition?"

Colorado lifted his head, smiled that spacy smile of his, and tossed some hair from his face.

"Nah, man, we're golden. You stress. We'll chill. And

then we'll see which approach is best," Colorado called, then returned to his songs.

"We're fucking doomed," Tate sighed, his notes becoming doodles of Team USA being kicked in the ass by Team China. The Chinese team had a big boot. Huge.

I glanced at the screen just in time to see Stan make crazy good save number twenty-four.

Yeah, we had our work cut out for us. And we'd not even seen Team Canada or any of the other teams compete yet.

Let the stressing begin.

The Beijing National Indoor Arena was packed, and most of the fans were hometown fans. Which was to be expected. We had a small contingency of backers, lots of family and friends who had flown over, as well as our fellow competitors from different events. Just as Jared and I had gone to watch luge this morning, some of the speed skaters were here to watch our game.

As we gathered in the locker room for one final pep talk from Coach Jamieson, I prayed we would give the US fans a good showing. I knew there were lots of mixed emotions about pro players being here and competing. Add in the fact that we had some vocally out and proud queer players on the roster, and emotions were high. We'd been treated cordially anywhere we went by the people of China, but any governmental faces we spied were always tinged with disapproval. So, I worked twice as hard to be four times as friendly. All eyes were on me, it felt.

My stress levels were through the roof after doing several hours of interviews, then a grueling team skate this morning. While we were highly favored to win this game, being cocky had been known to lead a team to a big fat loss.

I had to stay focused, pass when it was safe, and not take wild chances. Tate and I had played together years before, but we were rusty now. Coach felt that the lines would jibe as we advanced. He also thought a weaker team was a good warm-up for us.

"Work out the kinks now, before we move on to facing Canada in the next preliminary," Coach had said this morning, after putting us through our paces.

It felt odd not to start a game with the anthems. The larger European rinks also took some getting used to. Fifteen feet didn't sound like much, but it was. The neutral zone was wider—as well as the offensive, defensive, and crease zones. Size matters, as they say. You could have NHL players who struggled in the bigger rinks, as well as European players who rocked it on the big ice, then come over to North America and tank. It was all about adjusting, Coach kept telling us. Change kept us sharp, he repeated. All the changes in my life were doing the opposite. My head was so full of non-hockey shit that focusing on the game was challenging. Thankfully, my stressors hadn't crept into my brain yet. I did *not* need another episode of barf-on-your-roommate.

The opening face-off was easily won. I shuttled it to Dewey Lake, a great winger from Minnesota. He was short for a hockey player, but *man* was he fast. We sailed down the ice, passing neatly, angling around the Chinese defense with little resistance. Dewey shuttled the puck to me in front of the net. I hoisted my stick upward to try to deflect the puck. The Chinese goalie just got his shoulder up in time to block it. The rebound was fucking meaty. I pounced on it, jamming the puck at the leg pad of the Chinese goalie. He sealed his skate to the post. The puck was loose for a good five seconds, sticks poking at the frozen round of rubber, until it shot free and into the corner. Some soft checking took place to free the puck and send it to our end of the ice. My line skated off. Tate's rolled out.

I washed the lactic acid from my mouth, took a long drink of water, and watched Collins do his thing. The son-of-a-bitch was good. Always had been. Better than good, actually. He was Hall of Fame material. I'd left Dallas to try to get out from under his incredibly long shadow. And I had in Harrisburg. Coming here, I'd assumed Tate would be first line center, but Coach Jamieson had put him on the second line. He'd still made Tate captain, but that was a given because Tate was a hundred kinds of awesome and a leader in the locker room with his serious focus.

"I'm a wealthy man," the chubby sixty-year-old head coach from Dallas had told the press the day the team had arrived in Beijing. "We have so much talent on this team that it's hard to divvy up the greatness equally. Madsen-Rowe centering the first line and Collins centering the second spreads what I think are the two best centers in the league. Will that change? Perhaps. We'll see how they both perform."

Thankfully, Tate had seemed to have no issue with being second, given he was captain and all. And I was kind of jazzed to be on the first line. I'd spent a few years playing second fiddle to Collins. And while I liked him, I disliked being second banana.

The game wasn't going as I'd have liked. We were beating the Chinese team. The second period had seen two goals scored for Team USA—a nice wraparound by Collins early in the period, followed about a minute later with a blistering slapshot from Benton Willoughby, a winger from New Jersey, who was on our fourth line.

Colorado was having a light night of it. Only ten shots on goal in nearly forty minutes of play, and those were weak attempts at best. Going into the third period, I had to give the Chinese team kudos for playing a plucky game. They were giving it their all, but they were just outmatched by a team filled with NHL stars. About ten minutes into the third on a power play, I managed to pick up the puck at the middle after sailing untouched through the neutral zone, following a dump pass from China. I moved to the left, snaking around a Chinese defender; the defenseman was too far back to cover me as he should have. I snapped the puck off my stick. It sailed across all kinds of real estate, and their goalie missed picking it up—probably because of a screen from his own defenseman—the shot going high and over his left shoulder. He'd want that one back for sure. With a hoot, I threw my arms into the air. My teammates converged around me by the boards, patting my helmet, smiles wide.

That felt good. I'd gotten a goal. Some of the pressure was off for now. Looking up into the quiet stands, I found the Team USA fans waving their banners and American flags. It felt great. Pride and patriotism filled me.

"Guess that shows the world that gay men can play hockey," Dewey said as we made our way to the bench.

"Dude, I've been showing the world that for a few years now," I replied as I took another moment to soak up the atmosphere.

My first Olympic goal. Ten minutes later, I checked first Olympic win off my bucket too. We'd better enjoy the glory. Our next preliminary game was against Canada.

I suspected they'd be a whole different kettle of fish.

Chapter Seven

Jared

Russia had beaten Switzerland four to one, the US had jumped all over China and won five to nothing, and there was no reason to expect that Canada wouldn't beat Germany.

So, what the fuck was going wrong?

There wasn't one specific thing, and that was the most frustrating part. If we didn't pull our heads out of our asses in these last few minutes, we were going to lose our first game. Maybe we could be tighter in front of the net, maybe we needed to fight harder in the corners, maybe the defensemen weren't pulling their weight. I didn't know, but we were sloppy and losing by a goal with three minutes remaining. Maybe the team was waiting for Germany to make a mistake, but our opponents hadn't made a wrong step and were easily the better team today. Germany was a strong team, packed full of topflight NHL stars, and coming off the back of a strong showing in the last Olympics. We knew it wouldn't be easy.

Coach Devers tilted his board a little so that I could see, but he didn't have to show me to know what might have to happen next. Our only hope to get an edge and a possible decision was to take our goalie—a strong-looking Di Costa—off the ice, and get a forward out in play to have us six on five. Then, maybe, we'd be able to salvage this mess.

Ryker's line reached the bench, and I could see the way Ryker perched on the edge of his seat, desperate to get back out there. I was momentarily distracted and fighting the need to clap my hand to his shoulder in reassurance. It wasn't as if we even had a time out, we could use—hell, we'd used that ten minutes ago to try to get some passion on the ice, but it hadn't worked.

The crowd noise grew, and I followed the play as LeFleur shuttled the puck to Smith—a perfect pass that didn't jump or spin—Smith barely glancing at it and collecting it, as if they'd played together all their lives. The German goalie went out of his net, watching for the cross-net shot that he assumed would be coming, but with two minutes left on the clock, Smith slapped the hell out of the puck, and it soared right over the goalie's shoulder, smashing into the net. The Canadian contingent in the Wukesong Arena went wild, making more noise than at a home game in Harrisburg, and like that, we were at three goals each, and there was exactly one minute and fifty-seven seconds to go. Everyone out there jumped on Smith —Smith bro-hugged LaFleur, then swooped in a wide arc of celebration to our bench.

"Thank fuck," Devers muttered so only his coaches could hear, then louder, he yelled: "Attaboy." The team celebration was short—everyone ready for the next face-off—but not before the pep talk, which was mostly telling them to stand their ground. I didn't have to say anything to my defensemen. I nodded at them, then pinched my forefinger and thumb together, and they knew what I meant. Stay tight, stay close, don't dump the puck.

If this was a Hollywood movie, we'd score now. With seconds on the clock, there would be a near-impossible, heroic rush, and our heroes in the red and white would somehow get a puck past an impenetrable German defense, and we'd have that single wonderful goal.

It didn't happen.

There was no swell of music or last gasp goal—there was just a sad, solid tie, which meant we were heading into overtime and a five-minute four-on-four sudden death situation. The first team to score a goal taking the precious extra points.

Everyone focused on every word Coach Devers said. He was sending out Ryker alongside Smith, and part of me just wanted to grab Ryker and stop him to give him a pep talk, which was just stupid because he knew what he was doing. The team hit the ice with confidence, and I prayed to anyone who would listen that these last few minutes would give us that extra point because, otherwise, we'd be one step closer to having to fight just to stay in this damn competition. There was no Zamboni out to fix the ice between normal play and the overtime, we'd be out on the kind of ice we'd played on as kids—rough, torn-up, and a mess.

Smith won the face-off, LaFleur caught it, shuttled it to Ryker, and the play happened so fast I don't even think Germany had a chance to think, let alone react. One more slide, one more push, a lucky bounce of a defender's skate, and Smith had the puck, right at the net, Ryker open and waiting for a rebound in that split-second of opportunity. The shot was smooth, ricocheted from the German goalie's glove. Ryker caught it, slammed it at the net, but it hit the pipes, and my heart stopped. The Germans were all over Smith, a wall of sticks and men, but there was LaFleur, coming down the right side, fighting in the corner, collecting the puck, passing it back without looking. Smith angled his stick to deflect the puck to Ryker, but the angle was wrong, and Ryker had no choice but to skate it around the net for a wraparound, only this was exactly what needed to happen, as he caught the goalie on his edge. He had one chance, digging in, turning on a dime, and shooting the puck at the net.

The crowd went silent for a second and then erupted into groans from German fans and yells from the Canadians, as the puck went past the German goalie and hit the back of the net. The referee indicated it was a good goal in a quick movement, and the Canadian bench erupted.

We'd won that precious shining point, and we were second in Group A, after the USA.

As for me, I was busting with pride.

My son had done that.

We exchanged grins. I couldn't help it; I didn't want to be stoic. It was as good as us winning the goddamned gold. The celebrations were subdued—of course we were *pleased* that we'd won, but the fact it was in overtime meant that we were at a disadvantage, and it was only game one. It wasn't inevitable that Canada would top the table, nor that we'd even make it to the quarterfinals, whatever the pundits said when they put us as one of the three favorites. We had to take the win and run with it, but it was a sober group of coaches who were locked into Coach Dever's room. He was pacing, I was seated, and Oli was being all weird-ass goalie coach, but was the only one who could feel half-way relaxed after Di Costa's showing, even if he was stressed.

"This should have been a win in regulations," Devers repeated for what had to be the tenth time. "What the fuck happened?"

I winced internally. He'd asked us that several times before, and every time I opened my mouth to defend my guys, I shut it again. There was no defending the sloppy first period that had given Germany the edge and a two-goal lead in the space of two minutes. I could roll out all the stuff about how lack of practice time meant that the team wasn't a cohesive whole, but there was no point—we all knew that. I could mention that my guys were solid, but then I'd be lying because they'd been solid for about eighty percent of the game, and the other twenty had been a mess.

"I'm switching up Ryker to first line," Devers announced, and I glanced up in shock to see he was staring at me. Was he expecting me to react? Would it be a bad thing to punch the air with my fist and let out a whoop? Probably. "He showed incredible presence of mind in this game, older than his years, and I want him on the same line as Smith."

He was still staring at me, but after a pause, he focused on the goaltending, and his shock announcement—taking third-line Ryker and pushing him up, working with Smith, the acknowledged star of our team—was enough to have me alternating between pride and despair. I'd seen the pressure on Ten, knew that at times the weight of expectation was exhausting for my husband—did I want to see that on Ryker?

The meeting ended, and when we left the room, Ryker, Smith, and a couple of other forwards were leaning against the wall. I guessed they were waiting for their time with Coach Devers. They'd all looked as if they were expecting a dressing down—even Smith, who wouldn't meet my gaze—but I wanted to congratulate them all on a game well fought. Well, after I told them they'd fucked up in the first period. I said nothing. I tried not to smile, or grin, or grab my son and warn him. Instead, I stood to one side and let them in, then pulled the door behind them.

"Coffee?" Oli suggested, and gestured for me to follow. I wanted to phone Ten, have him tell me it was all okay, and at the same time, I didn't want to put him in that position. He'd been so high after the win this morning, and I'd taken his joy with me to our game—then had lost it in the space of a few minutes. I wasn't in the right headspace to talk to my husband, and I readily agreed to a coffee, which was code for an off-the-record chat with a fellow coach.

That was what I needed. Ten would understand, and I refused to glance at my phone, which had vibrated with several messages, because I might just call him and lay all my anxieties, and my pride, and my general confusion, on my poor husband's shoulders. He deserved to enjoy his win. Oli and I took our drinks to a quiet corner with cozy sofas and not a single hockey player in sight. We could have gone back to our room, but I guess neither of us were ready to do that yet. A figure skater hurried past, taking time to congratulate us on the win, high fiving both of us and leaving a trail of sequins, but other than that, we were alone.

"That was brutal," Oli murmured, and I sighed because this wasn't going to be some self-congratulatory chat where we glossed over our mistakes.

"Yeah, too many turnovers, too much…" Too much of everything we didn't want to see in a hockey game. "Thank fuck we had Di Costa." I felt as if I should apologize for the way the defense had fallen to bits in front of Di Costa, and for that first twenty minutes we'd been lucky to only allow two goals.

"He's solid," Oli agreed. 'Good news about…" He waved his fingers, and I assume he meant about Ryker. "You must be proud."

I smiled then, allowing myself a moment of being a father. "Proud, scared, in awe of his talent." Then I cleared my throat. "Okay, let's dissect this."

And we did, and it was painful, and by the time we'd finished, I felt halfway better. In two days, we were meeting the US, and I at least had a workable solution to go up against the powerhouses of Ten and Tate.

Not one that would necessarily work, but a solution, nonetheless.

Oli headed off to do whatever goalie coaches did, and I went back to our room, meeting Ryker, who was coming to find me, sporting the widest grin. I tugged him in before he could speak, and for the longest time, I hugged him so hard. We called his mom, and we enjoyed every moment of Ryker's success.

"So proud of you," I said as he left, probably the twentieth time I'd said that in the space of twenty minutes.

"Thanks, Dad." He checked his watch. "It's Jacob time!"

"Give him my love."

"I will." We fist-bumped then, an acknowledgment of everything—of the win, the goal, and his news. After he left, I knew I wanted to speak to Ten, but it took me another half hour of getting my head straight before I thumbed to his number and sent him a text asking if he was free to talk.

He called me immediately.

"Hey, you," he said with a smile in his voice, and that was enough to settle me. "Congratulations on the win," he added, and I could picture his genuine smile. "Are you coming over, or do you want me to come to you?"

Jeez, I wanted to. I needed a Ten-hug right about now, but I wasn't in a good place, all messed up inside, with the near loss, and then with Ryker.

"I'm exhausted," I muttered and rolled over to my side, staring out into the night as Ten rambled on about the US being best. I wanted to tell him so much about Ryker, only I shouldn't, because that could give the US team a heads-up on strategizing a new defense. But Ten wouldn't go running to the coaches, right? I wanted to share the pride with my husband, a man who loved Ryker.

"Can I tell you something in confidence?" I asked softly.

He chuckled. "Always. Colorado's not here right now —he's off saving emus or something. Did you know the trains here are called EMUs? That's sent him off doing fuck knows what. Oh, and Stan has decided he likes emus as well. Freaking goalies, it's all in the Railers chat when you get there, but it's some funny shit."

I hadn't even looked at the chat since the game. Maybe I needed to do that? Catch up with Stan, who never failed to make me smile, but Stan and Ten were both winners, and Team Canada had scraped through. How could I—

"Babe? Are you okay?" Ten interrupted my stupidity.

"Yeah, Ryker—"

"Shit, that goal was amazing. I was on the edge of my seat, and when he got it home, I was up and shouting, and Tate had to calm me down. It's kind of weird I can root for the opposition, right?" He huffed a laugh.

"Coach is pushing him up to first line with Smith. I'm so proud." Sharing about Ryker was the right thing to do, and for the first time since our game against Germany had ended, I felt that it was okay to be proud of Ryker, and to share that with Ten.

Silence. Then Ten sniffed. "Oh fuck, now I'm crying. Our boy…"

"Yeah."

Chapter Eight

Ten

There are some unwritten rules in life.

Like don't hit on your best friend's lover, always put the toilet seat down, and make sure you don't say something bad in front of your children unless you want them to repeat the cuss word in public or to your mother. There are a lot of others as well, for sure. Looking up from the most delicious Peking Duck I had ever tasted, I spotted Team Finland entering the Lemon Grove Restaurant, one of the top-rated places to eat near the Olympic Village. The rich flavor of duck combined with the salty/sweet hoisin sauce with sharp green onion soured on my tongue. Aarni was smiling at something one of his teammates had said as he divested himself of his blue and white team jacket. It took all I had to force that bite of duck down. Fucker. Fucking fuck fucker.

I'd been so careful in trying to avoid him. I'd shut down the ten million questions about the past from the press corps with the standard—*"I'm here to play hockey and represent my country." "What happened is the past and is not affecting me in the least." "I wish him and Team Finland well."*—tag lines the team had directed me to use. But what did I say to my teammates now? While sitting in a packed eatery with the world watching me battle back barfing.

"I have to use the men's room," I said after choking down my food.

Tate glanced up from his meal, as did Colorado, Carter, and the other six men who'd dragged me out of my room to see the Mutianyu section of the Great Wall of China. Which had been incredible. Now the whole day was ruined. Great. Loved this trip for me. The sites should not include the bastard who'd nearly ended my career as well as my life. Fucker.

Keeping my pace slow—streaking to the bathroom was the default—I entered the men's room, whispered a thank-you to whoever was listening that it was empty, and bent over a sink. My food rose into my throat. Eyes squeezed shut, I burped and swallowed, swallowed, and burped, until my duck went back down. My gaze lifting from the sink, I studied my face. Man, I looked like total shit.

The door opened, and Colorado sauntered in, all Hollywood-pretty and totally unruffled by anything. Why would he be? What had he faced in his charmed life to upset him?

"Had a duck bone caught in my throat," I lied.

"Troubling times," he replied, his gaze roaming over my clammy face. "You okay?"

"Sure, yeah. Why wouldn't I be?" The words snapped

like a rubber band wound too tightly. "I mean why would I be not okay? I'm only carrying the weight of every fucking LGBTQ player on my back, as well as the expectations of my country. My baby cries every time we have to say goodbye. My husband is in another building. And my roommate stepped right out of Steely Dan! The world is fucking fine. Peaches and cream!"

I threw myself into a stall just so I wouldn't have to see his smiling face. What was the jackass grinning at? I'd just called him a hippie. Which now that I had my brow on the cool metal door, I realized was a shitty dig. "Sorry, man. I'm on edge."

He grinned. "I will gladly take the Steely Dan callout. Did you know that Don Fagan and Walter Becker were jazz enthusiasts, who weren't even into rock until they heard "Ticket to Ride" from The Beatles?"

My head was starting to throb. "I did not know that."

"Truth. So hey, here's something for you to ponder on as you drop a duke. Are you tuning into me in there?"

I sighed. "Yeah, I hear you."

"Cool. So, my thing for you to contemplate is this. You don't have to carry the weight of every queer athlete competing here." I squeezed my eyes shut; my lips pressed tight. "I mean, no one asked you to represent us all, right? I don't think I did. I'm totally down with keeping tabs on myself and my sexuality with the media. It's righteous and fucking admirable that you feel you have to shoulder that burden for all of us hockey players, or even all the LGBTQ athletes, but you really don't. We're good at carrying our own weight. Also, Lankinen is a total spiked cock cage, and he *will* be dealt with on the ice. We got this. *We*. Note that I'm using a term that means more than just you. Your team will have your back. You don't have to shoulder that alone either."

I blew out a shaky breath and he paused for a moment.

"So yeah, that's all I wanted to tell you," he added. "Now, I'm going to go order us some more tea, then lead the guys over to the Summer Palace. Maybe you should see if your husband is free for an hour or two. The room will be empty."

He patted the stall door.

"Okay," I croaked, feeling like a mound of freshly deposited dog shit. I unlocked the door and peered through the crack. Colorado was standing there, worn jeans, Aerosmith tee under his team jacket, wild long hair pulled back into a ponytail, lips curled into a warm smile. "Thanks, Colorado. For the talk. And for being cool."

"Dude, I am Steely Dan cool. That is incredibly cool." He patted my cheek, then ambled back out of the door. I let the stall door close, leaned my ass to it, and pulled out my cell. Jared answered on the first ring.

"Hey, baby," he said, and the heaviness on my shoulders lessened considerably. It was amazing what just hearing his voice could do to me. "Everything okay?"

"You got anything going for the next hour or two?"

There was a slight pause. I chastised myself for even calling him. He had a ton of work to do, obviously; we were all under enormous pressure to perform.

"Nothing that can't wait. Saw your Instagram post at the Great Wall. Wish we could have seen that together."

"We will. After we win the gold medal, I'll take you there."

He snickered softly. "You mean after you win the silver. You okay?"

"I could use some *us-time* to be honest. Ran into Lankinen. Totally soured my Peking Duck."

"Shit. How long will it take you to get to the Olympic Village?"

"Twenty minutes tops."

"Okay, I'll sneak in and be waiting for you outside your door."

"Sneaking in with a big old red maple leaf on your back?"

"Hey, I'm all about the stealth."

He so totally wasn't. "I'll meet you at my door. Don't get caught sneaking around. You know how much Snape hates when we do that."

He chuckled. "I'll do my best to avoid Snape."

He ended the call. I snuck out, saw that my team was still sipping tea, and made my excuses, citing an upset stomach. With a wink from Colorado, I tossed some cash onto the table, slid my arms into my star-spangled jacket, and walked out, ignoring the looks from Team Finland as I neared their table.

"Good luck," I said as I passed by. Aarni watched me intently, but kept his mouth shut. The others on his team returned my good wishes.

I stepped out into the cool air, got my bearings, then hailed a cab. My Mandarin was atrocious, but I got the destination across somehow. Traffic was a gnarl. I willed the cab to move.

It couldn't go fast enough to get me into Jared's arms.

Stepping out of the elevator, I spied Mr. Conspicuous right off the bat. And smiled widely.

Jared glanced up from his phone, his blue eyes soft and warm.

"Didn't even try to hide all that Canada, eh?" I asked as I walked down the hall.

"Nope." He popped the *P* then opened his arms. I stepped directly into his embrace, his scent immediately calming my jangled nerves. "What happened, babe?"

"Can we go inside?"

He nodded. I scanned my key card, stepped through the door, and tossed my team jacket to the bed. Jared followed me in, making soft clucking noises.

"Wow, he's a little scattered," Jared commented, his gaze raking over the chaos that was Colorado's side of the room.

"He tells me that a creative mind cannot be burdened by the weight of a Swiffer or a dustpan," I tossed out as I toed off my sneakers.

"Obviously, his mind is greatly unencumbered."

I plastered myself to him, sliding my arms around his middle, rubbing my lips over the short blond and silver bristles on his cheek. I loved that abrasion. He cinched me close. I leaned into a thick length of something delicious in his front pocket.

"Is that a banana in your pocket or are you just glad to see me?" I teased, eager to forget the encounter with Aarni by flooding my head with mind-blowing sex.

"Oh, shit, yeah it is." I pulled back a bit, confused as

hell, as he reached into his front pocket and withdrew a banana. "I wasn't sure how you'd be feeling and saw a fruit bowl on my way from the video room, so…"

He placed the somewhat bruised fruit into my hand. "And you thought this would do what for me exactly?"

He shrugged. "Maybe some extra potassium would make you feel better?"

"You're such a doofus," I said then laughed, tossing the banana to my nightstand. "I'll eat that later. Right now, I need to have you in me. That's what will make me feel better. Please, Jared."

"Okay, babe, I've got you." He kissed me lovingly, but hotly, his tongue staking his claim as I yanked at his clothing. I was desperate to have him. To purge the crap that was Aarni from my skull with something good and strong and miraculous. Our clothes flew to the four corners, his hands roaming over my sides, clutching my ass as he tasted my mouth over and over. He took a step, I did as well, and my calves hit my neatly made bed. Down onto the concrete mattress we went, his hips settling between my splayed legs. "Shit, we need lube. Do you have any?"

"I have a banana," I replied, then waved a hand at said fruit.

"You really want to use banana paste as lubricant?" He nipped at my jawline as he spoke, his fat cockhead probing at my hole, pre-cum slicking things a little, but not nearly enough.

"No, not really. In my bag."

He jumped up. I let my eyes close, breathing in the scent of his cologne as it lingered in the air. Then he was back, his right hand coming to rest on my stomach as his left probed under my balls. A gasp fluttered out of me when his slick fingers breached me.

"You do know that fucking is all well and good, but we're going to talk about what happened with Aarni after we're done." He was so bossy. I nodded, my eyes opening slowly, then locking with his. His expression softened. "I love you so much at times that even thinking of him near you again makes me…"

"Ragey?"

"Yes."

"Then stop thinking about him for a little bit. Make love to me."

I reached for him, arching up to get more of his fingers. With a grunt that sounded like surrender, he kissed my knees, then replaced his fingers with his cock. Easing in, working himself deeper and deeper with each flick of his hips. Cocooned by his love, I felt freed from the worries of the world, even if just for a short time, the weight was gone. And all that remained was me, Jared, and the joining of our bodies and hearts. He moved with a knowledge of what I loved the most—his hips rolling, his cock sliding over my prostate time and time again. I held tight to his forearms; my gaze locked with his as his speed increased. He took hold of my bouncing cock, stroked it a few times, and then went so deep my breath left my body. My orgasm hit me hard, like a blind bodycheck that smears your face into the glass. Cock pulsing, I cried out. He fell over me, pressing his mouth to mine to smother the cries of passion. I drove my heels into his ass, clenched tight, and was instantly rewarded with a flood of cum painting me inside.

"Ah hell," he groaned, his brow on mine, his eyes screwed shut as he rode out his release. I watched him throughout, amazed at how glorious he was when he came. When his eyes flickered open, I smiled at him. "That was incredible."

He kissed my cheeks, my nose, my chin, and then finally, my puffy lips. I wrapped myself around him like a vine, keeping him inside as long as possible, not wanting to let this tenderness slip away and be replaced by the real world. The real world sucked.

"You're so good," I sighed as my muscles relaxed. We melted into the bedding, him easing out when it was impossible to stay buried in me. I moaned at the loss of his prick, but lay there unmoving as I floated back to reality.

He sat up, found his shirt, and wiped up before handing it to me.

"What will you wear back to your room?"

"I'll borrow something of yours and zip up the jacket to my chin so as not to expose my traitorous colors," he answered as he stretched out beside me.

"Benedict Arnold," I whispered as I shoved his T-shirt between my legs. I'd make sure it went to the laundry service with my clothes and get it back to him. Or maybe I'd keep it. Everyone needed a Team Canada tee.

"That's an American traitor. We have Joseph Willocks," he informed me as he placed a hand to my chest and began to rub between my pecs.

"*Who?*"

"War of 1812. Switched sides mid-war to fight for the

Americans. Created a regiment that spied on their fellow Canadians still loyal to the British."

"Gasp. Damn them Americans and their temptations."

"Indeed." He bent to place his lips to my shoulder. "So, what happened with Aarni? Word for word. I want to know if I need to go find him in a dark alley."

"No dark alleys please," I asked, reveling in the cooling of my body and the soft touch of my husband's hand. "It was nothing. He said nothing, barely glanced at me. I just had a huge PTSD reaction to his face. It was over-the-top. My stress levels are jacked. I'll get it under control."

He stared down at me, his head resting in his hand, short blond hair sweaty at his hairline. He looked well-fucked. It was a great look for him.

"You burden yourself with far too much, sweetheart."

"Yeah, Colorado said the same thing." I wiggled to my side. "Can we just spend some time cuddling?"

He nodded, let his head drift to my pillow, then gathered me close. I yanked the covers up, buried my nose in his neck, and simply breathed in Jared.

Chapter Nine

Jared

Facing off against Team USA was daunting, terrifying, and exciting. There was nothing I could do—I'd discussed strategy with my guys, talked to Oli about putting Di Costa in next, and we could talk until we were blue in the face about the mechanics of how to defend against the likes of Ten and Tate, and still come up short.

There was no set way to stop them from scoring, and I knew that from personal experience, watching in awe of my husband at every Railers' game, and watching the Railers' defenseman struggling against Tate whenever we met the Raptors. Coach Devers was giving the final speech, but he was uncharacteristically quiet and firm, with very little bluster or fiery passion.

"… keep it tight, don't take your eye off the puck for a single second. I want crisp line changes, no penalties, and remember their superstars use the bathroom the same way we do—they're not superhuman."

"Not sure Ten and Tate are human," someone muttered —I think it was Smith—and a couple of the guys added their soft *amens* before glancing at me.

I didn't know what they expected me to say or do now. Did they want me to join in? Or tell them secrets that would give them an edge? There was no way in hell I'd use my inside knowledge of Ten's headspace right now to give Canada an opening. When I'd left him, he'd been in a good place, and we'd texted as much as we could. Before this game, he'd texted me good luck with twenty-five added hearts, and when I texted back I sent twenty-six, with a grinning emoji. If we won clean today, then it would even the playing field, and if Germany then went on to beat the US in their game, we might even get top of the table.

Easy, right?

"… and that's what we need, focus."

Ironically, I wasn't focused in that moment, but I nodded along with everyone else. Then, it was all about getting out on the ice. I watched our team as they warmed up, and tried not to follow Ten as he skated in lazy circles around the net, passing to another player, never once aiming for the goalie. I focused on Ryker, watched him skate toward center line and catch Ten's eye. They fist-bumped right there, and I could tell from this distance that there was chirping, and I wondered if it was my son or my husband who came off best in that one. From Ten's grin and Ryker's smirk, I genuinely couldn't tell. All I could think was I was glad Ryker hadn't followed in my skates to become a defenseman, because then he'd be up against Ten in the worst kind of way.

Devers, Oli, and I took the space between warmups and game to talk in low tones about how skaters looked, how they stood on the ice, about the uniforms—USA in blue on white and Canada in white on scarlet—and hell, anything else we could think of that might give us an edge. Canada were the favorites here, even though we'd missed the very high benchmark set for us in the Germany game, but the US had power names. No one in their right minds could call it, even if they were forced to come down for either team. The tension in the stadium was high, and the start, with Ten taking a face-off against Smith, was pitting two of the best against each other.

The two teams were even, both of us getting a goal past determined goalies in the second period, both teams having perfect shining moments when everything seemed to be going right. The number of shots on goal was insanely high, but the goalies were hot, and there was nothing splitting the teams. When the US team had possession, our defense was solid, when we were in control, the US was never far from our skates. Ryker held his own, Smith was a beast, Ten was a god, Tate was a genius, and adrenaline rushed through me so intensely that I was shaky with it.

This was going to go into overtime—I could see the inevitability of it as Smith headed up-ice, blocked by the US defense, and passed back to Ryker who was checked into the Plexi-glass so hard I swore it would give way. I waited for him to fall, but he didn't; he somehow stayed on his skates, and miraculously the puck was in the corner, and Ryker was right in the thick of it. He managed to get it free, and scooted it back with a blind pass, trusting one of his team would at least be there. All the puck found was the waiting US defense, but it hit one of their D-men on the shin, bounced in the opposite direction, skittered on the ice, and the only one there to collect it was Smith, who didn't hesitate to use every ounce of his skill and power, and shoot hard at Colorado. He was caught off guard by the bounce and reacted just a hair too late.

For a second no one could understand what had happened, but with only thirty-seven seconds to go, somehow in a moment of technicolor glory, Smith had found the back of the net, and we were up two goals to their one.

The last few seconds were a masterclass in keeping the puck away from the US team, even though they had Ten and Tate out on the ice *and* pulled their goalie. They wanted us to waver—we didn't.

When the final buzzer sounded and we'd won, I hugged everyone near me, from Oli to Devers, to DK the skate guy, and the young kid with the boxes of drinks, who had hovered near us all through the game.

The high of beating the US was like winning the freaking Stanley Cup.

The win was everything to the team—a check next to our name, and on points, we were top of the table, with the US and Germany next at three points each, and China with zero. If we could beat China, and there was no reason not to, then we'd booked our place in the next round.

That was worth celebrating, although the half smile Ten sent me held so much disappointment that I wanted to throw caution to the wind and run over to him and hug it all out so he felt better.

"Don't do it," Oli muttered under his breath and gripped my arm.

"I wasn't going to," I lied.

"Yes, you were," he pointed out with a squeeze. "Let's go do this celebrating thing."

I caught up with Ryker when he was showered and dressed, and he was grinning like a Cheshire cat. "We won!" He high-fived me, and then we hugged like only family can do, with joyous abandon and a ton of love. It was just one more game on the way to the final, but I got a feeling in my bones that maybe—just maybe—Canada could do this thing.

Oli and I headed back to our room, but as if by unspoken agreement, he didn't come in for long—just enough time to grab a lighter jacket and his tablet. I didn't know if he was deliberately heading out so that I had the chance to talk to Ten, but I thanked him anyway. Privacy to speak freely would be hard to find out there in Team Canada land, particularly when a Canadian coach wanted to get all serious with an American skater. I fell on my phone and saw the one text I needed, *here when you are.*

I connected to Ten, and he answered so fast that he must have been waiting.

"Shit, J! Congratulations!" he said immediately, his voice filled with that beautiful smile. "Did you see that pass from Ryker? That kid is getting better every day. I'm so proud of him."

"Tennant—"

"And that deke in the first period when he—"

"Ten, stop."

"What?"

"I'm sorry, babe." I kept my tone gentle, and I heard his quiet sigh.

"It's all good, the game was intense."

"I know. How's Colorado doing?"

"He's angry as hell with himself and won't listen when I tell him it wasn't his fault. He's locked himself in the bathroom with his iPad to call home."

"It was a lucky bounce; he has to understand that, right? It could have gone either way."

"Don't do that," Ten murmured. "Don't spend time commiserating with us, when we played so well, and when you freaking won. I want to celebrate your success, okay?"

"And I want to be there for you right now."

Ten chuckled. "This rivals thing is shit, isn't it."

"Just a bit."

"I'm so proud of Ry," he said again, and pride for him was our middle ground between winning and losing, and not being there to hug each other.

"Me too."

"You know what, Jared?"

"What?"

"Being a stepdad is pretty freaking awesome."

"Being a dad and married to a stepdad-sort-of-brother-type person, is also awesome," I deadpanned.

We talked about everything and nothing, and there was one piece of common ground between us both knowing professional hockey—losing was felt just as keenly as winning, but there was always the next game. The medal race was far from over, and there was every chance that the

US would come out on top, or Canada, or hell—any one of the many good teams that were here. This wasn't just a USA/Canada race; after all, the Russian skaters had won all three of their games and were not only top of their group, but the best team right now. They were on fire, backstopped by the amazing brick wall that was Stan, and with so many big names in their team we'd be hard-pressed to slide easily past them.

"I'm going to make a move; Colorado is standing right next to me," Ten said after an hour of us discussing next year's vacation, Lottie, birds, Lottie, squirrels, Lottie, cheese, in fact *anything* but hockey, and agreeing that we missed our daughter too much to ever leave her again.

Ever.

"Does he have his junk out?" I joked—after all, for Colorado it appeared to be a default setting.

"He's too sad," Ten said and chuckled, then let out a loud yelp, as if Colorado had poked at him.

"That you, *Canuck*?" Colorado said, clearly having gotten the cell from Ten.

"Yep."

"Lucky bounce," Colorado stated in a way that I couldn't argue with, even if I didn't agree with him.

"Yep, that's the way it goes sometimes."

"We're coming for you," he threatened in his best gangster impression, and then snorted a laugh. "Don't ever think I'm coming to one of your barbecues again. I carry grudges a long time."

"Give me back the damn phone!" Ten said, and there was a loud scuffle. "Hey, you still there?"

"I'm here."

"He's an idiot."

"He's a goalie," I said, because that explained everything.

"I love you."

"I love you, too."

"Congratulations."

"Thank you, Ten. And I'm sorry that—"

"No more of that. We'll talk later."

"Later."

I stared at my phone for the longest time—at the screen lock photo of Ten and Lottie, then opened my gallery to find more photos of Ten, Lottie, Ryker, Jacob, the people in my life who made everything real. I missed Lottie worse than I ever imagined, worse than when we were on an away trip, where she was still on the same continent at least. What would happen when she was older? Would she get lonely? Maybe she needed a sibling. A kid brother or sister to boss around? Maybe after the Olympics, Ten and I should revisit our chats about extending the family. We were good dads, and we had a ton of love to give any child we had in our lives—maybe a teenager, after all I'd lived through the Ryker teenage years and had come out the other side intact. Ten and I could do anything together— achieve bigger things than just hockey.

I might have been on the winning team today, but in life, Ten and I were both winners.

———

We beat China, which put us at the top of our group, and into the quarterfinals. We could get a break for a while.

Then, Team USA beat Germany, but even two wins for them couldn't stop the fact that Switzerland, over in group C, had better stats and could well steal fourth place to go through to the quarterfinals automatically. Team USA may have to fight for a place in the next round, but it wasn't set in stone who'd they'd match up with. At least, not until the result of Finland facing Sweden was known. It was the only time I'd ever prayed that Aarni would get a win, because then Finland wouldn't need to fight the US for a place going forward. *Fight* being the operative word. I know Ten had said he wanted to face Aarni on the ice, but I couldn't help the icy grip of terror that held me whenever I imagined the two of them up against each other.

I'd nearly lost Ten.

Finland lost their game, and my blood ran cold, because Finland—and Aarni—were going to have to fight, just the same as the USA, to get to the next round. I held onto the hope that it didn't mean the US would be playing Finland for the coveted spot.

Only, when all the games were played, and everything was sorted into place, that was *exactly* what was going to happen.

USA vs Finland was the next game.

Ten vs Aarni.

Chapter Ten

Ten

The morning of the first quarterfinal game for Team USA dawned bleak. The weather outside was dull and wet, the skies heavy with rain. I'd not slept well and had shot up in my bed around three in the morning, doused in sweat, the vestiges of a familiar nightmare clinging to me. I was back in the hospital, unable to speak, my brain swollen, my loved ones gathered around watching me. A death watch. Of course, they'd not said as much, but I'd been able to see the fear in their eyes. Mom wept. Dad paced. Jared sat by my side, gripping my hand, telling me all would be well. And it had been… eventually. Back then, Jared and I had been childless. What kind of fresh hell would it be to see your child weeping over you as you hovered near a vegetative state? A shudder ran over me as I stared at the raindrops pelting the window.

Those first days after the head injury had been harrowing. I still could not put into words how terrifying it was not being able to speak or think properly. To not be able to recall common words such as water or pencil or shoe. How to draw a blank when you're asked to tie your shoe. Tying your shoe. Fuck, I'd learned that when I was four. I'd probably been tying hockey skates instead of shoes. To this day, there were times when I couldn't remember a word or perform simple math, although they were few and far between. Of course, there were the headaches as well, which were no fun. At all.

My head was a cause of concern. I got scans on a regular basis. Every concussion caused damage. It was a known fact, and something athletes in contact sports were fully aware of going in. A concussion from an errant check or a bad fall was one thing. To be slew-footed on purpose. Yeah, that was something else altogether different. That was one human being trying to destroy another human being. That was what Aarni Lankinen had done to me. And today, I'd be facing the man who had tried to do grievous bodily harm to me on the ice. I was at once scared shitless and eager to get this final confrontation over with. Needless to say, my head was a sloppy stew at the moment and I—

"You play guitar?"

Colorado's voice right beside my ear made me jump. I spun to face him. He was all geared up in his red, white, and blue USA street gear. I was in a pair of sleeping shorts.

"Uhm no. Piano. I play piano." I reached up to scrub my chin, the whiskers rough on my fingers.

"Oh, excellent. Makes it a little trickier, but where there's a will there's a way. Get dressed. I have an idea."

He began poking at his cell phone, long hair dangling in his face.

"I'm not sure I'm in the right head space to—"

"You'll thank me." He glanced up from his phone. "Trust me. I'm a goalie. I know all about treating funky head space situations. True?"

"Uhm. I guess?"

He chuckled, then grinned at his cell phone. "You know it to be true. Come on, get dressed. I got us a space to unwind properly."

Giving the rocker a suspicious look, I nonetheless pulled on some clothing from the monumental pile of stuff in the corner of the room. Colorado led me outside. The dampness settled on my shoulders quickly. We jumped into a cab. Colorado rattled off something in Mandarin, then gave me a wink.

"Took a crash course before coming over. My man helped. He's wickedly smart."

I nodded as we cruised along. The city of Beijing was fascinating. I wished I had more time to explore it properly. Maybe, someday, Jared, Lottie, and I could return. When she was older, so she'd appreciate the trip. Hell, maybe Jared and I would have more kids by then. I was totally open to that option. Being a father was the single most amazing thing I had ever done or would do.

"Right, so here we are!" Colorado shouted, taking me by the wrist and literally dragging me out of the tiny yellow cab. I tossed some renminbi at the driver, thanked him in dismal Mandarin, and then stumbled along behind Colorado into a musical instrument shop. The owner, a small Chinese man with silver hair, bowed as he let us in, then locked the door.

"What the hell is going on here?" I asked after thanking the owner a few more times.

"We're going to jam a little bit." Colorado slipped the man some red paper money, then waved at a beautiful piano. "I rented the store for an hour. Oh damn, that is one fine Epiphone Hummingbird!"

"What? No. We have to get to the ice to—"

"Tennant, buddy, amigo, chill. Honestly, you're too tight. Lankinen is living in your head space. You need to spend some time with the arts, playing a song or two will take you out of yourself. Trust me. Goalie head, remember?" He tapped his temple, then jogged over to a wall filled with acoustic and electric guitars. I threw a look at the owner, who was sitting on a stool behind the cash register sipping tea. He smiled at me. I smiled back. No help there. I glanced around the shop. They had a wide selection of instruments from tubas to electric guitars. I recalled reading that classical music was quite popular in China, so this great selection of orchestral instruments wasn't unusual at all in a country that loved the classics.

With nowhere else to go, and no other way to purge Aarni from my *"brain space,"* I sat at the gleaming black Steinway and ran my fingers over the keys. The tinkling ivories made me smile. I didn't play nearly as much as my mother would have liked. What with hockey and marriage and a baby, sitting down at the keys to simply play had fallen by the wayside. I did a quick warm-up, pulling a grin from Colorado as he sat beside me on the bench and proceeded to tune the cherrywood guitar in his hands.

"How sweet is our sound?"

"We're not bad."

"You're okay. I'm fucking stellar." That made me snicker. "You know any Beatles songs?"

"Sure. A few."

"Cool. See if you can keep up." He turned to the side, his back to my arm, and began strumming the opening stanza of "Get Back" until I could pick things up and play along. His voice was much better than mine, gruff and grumbly, just like a metal singer's should be. Noting that I was no Billy Preston, I filled in damn well, our voices blending nicely on choruses. The owner of the shop began clapping along, his head bobbing in perfect rhythm.

We ripped through a good two dozen songs ranging from "Love Me Do" to "I Am the Walrus," with a ripping metallic rendition of "Hey Jude" that Colorado recorded on his phone to share online to all his fans. Head bent over the keyboard, fingers dancing over the keys, I led us into "Here Comes the Sun" even though it was pouring outside.

"Okay, we have like five minutes left before Mr. Dan has to open to the public. Let's go out on this one," Colorado said, shoving his phone into the front pocket of his tattered jeans. "Make sure you feel the lyrics. These guys didn't pen fluff shit. Take in the words. Let them lead you." He nudged me in the side.

I nodded, waiting for our finale. When he began to pluck out "Let it Be," I jumped in, smoothly. He stopped playing, turned to face the keys, and just sang. As the song took us away, I let the words sink in. *Really* sink in. And I came to see that what I needed to do was just that. I had to let it be. Let the past be the past. Stop dwelling on it and the pain that I'd been through. That was done and over. There was no rewind. I had to focus forward. Play my game, live my life, and love the people around me. It was time to let it go.

When the final keys had been hit, Colorado and I exchanged looks. I nodded. He smiled.

Mr. Dan jumped to his feet to applaud.

"Thanks; this really helped," I said to Colorado.

"Surely it did. There is no ailment that music cannot heal. Shall we go make hockey now?"

"Let's do that."

We fist-bumped, signed some sheet music for Mr. Dan, and left the shop feeling a thousand pounds lighter. Or perhaps that was just me...

The vibe in the US locker room was tense when I arrived. Glancing around, I couldn't help but think that the place looked as if Captain America had blown up all over the players. You couldn't swing a stick without rapping it into some big guy in red, white, and blue.

My teammates were all staring at me with expectation. Colorado ambled in, humming something from Metallica as I gave everyone a nod and a smile.

"Right, so, we spent the morning jamming as you all saw on Instagram, I'm sure," I opened with. All the guys nodded, some made comments that earned them a middle finger from our goalie. "I'm really ready to put all the crap with Lankinen behind me. Let's just go out, play our game, and win one for the good old US of A!"

They cheered and grunted just like Tim "The Toolman"

Taylor from *Home Improvement*. The tension lessened considerably, and I had to wonder if it had been me and my shit that had cast a pallor over the team and our play. I vowed to do better for the men gathered here.

Coach Jamieson showed up ten minutes before warm-ups. His speech was short and to the point as they had always been. Play hard, play smart, leave the personal stuff in the locker room. His steely gaze met mine. I inclined my head. Message received. I was on that shit. I made double sure to follow all my good luck routines. Left skate on first, then right. Stick taping while I listened to "*Astoria*," a Marianas Trench album I always listened to while taping my stick. Hockey players were big on routine. And as we were in a strange country, playing in a strange barn, with strange rink dimensions, we'd need all the luck we could get.

All was chill, as Colorado would say, until we hit the ice for warm-ups. Looking across the rink, I spied Aarni making lazy circles, flicking the puck at the empty net, talking amiably with one of the other men in the blue jerseys. His eyes lifted and met mine. Tate was chattering to me about something when I skated off, intending to meet him at center ice. We came close once, then lapped again, and the second time I slowed to a stop. He did the same.

"Did you want something from me, Rowe?" Aarni asked. I extended my hand. His eyes flared. I imagined ten thousand pictures being snapped as I waited, my skates on one side of the red line, his on the other. "What's this?"

"This is me saying I forgive you."

There was no mistaking the shock. His head jerked

back slightly, and his mouth fell open. Other players slowed around us, most coming to a stop, my team backing me and his backing him.

"I don't need your forgiveness for an accident," he stated, his eyes darting to the other Finnish players. What they were thinking, I couldn't say, but I'd played with and against several of them, and knew most to be good, clean players. "I know what you are doing. Trying to make me look the bad guy." With that low growl, he slapped his hand into mine. His grip was punishing. I squeezed back just as hard.

"Think what you want. Just know that you're forgiven." And just like that I let it be. I released his hand, turned, and found several hulking men staring at me. I skated off, as did Aarni, my team saying nothing, but moving in close as if saying they approved and had my back. Which would prove to be good, because as soon as the puck dropped the Finns were on us like ugly on an ape, to quote my father.

Play was fast and physical. Little scoring was taking place as both teams churned out hard defensive play. The head coaches had to be thrilled. Tate and I were being shut down as soon as we entered the neutral zone, and so were their top forwards. At the end of the first period, Team Finland had four shots and we had five. Nothing was making it to the net. During the intermission, Coach Jamieson was as happy as a clam, telling us to keep playing as we were. The Finns would make a mistake that we could capitalize on, he was sure.

"Keep protecting the net. Keep giving a hundred percent. You know they're going to come out and give that much. So now we see what we're made of. I know you're tired. I know you've got bruises. I know you have the skills to put this game away. Keep shooting. I don't care if most of the shots get blocked. All it takes is one to get through. One shot, one goal, one game at a time. We can do this."

Coach Jamieson always gave good speeches. We hit the ice with a fury. The play increased in intensity. Maybe the Finnish coach had also given a good speech, because the Finns gave us all we could handle and then some. My ass hit the ice and the boards a hundred times. Jarring checks that rattled fillings. Most coming from Lankinen, but not all. The Finnish defense was massive. It was like trying to knock a sequoia over when going into the corners. Still, we hung tough and battled things out until there was a little over two minutes left in the second period. Exhausted, sore, and getting cranky, we lined up for a face-off to the left of the Finnish goal. Tate was facing off against the Finnish captain. Aarni slid up next to me, his elbow knocking into mine.

"The brave eats the soup," he said.

I threw him a look. "We're talking soup?"

He chuckled before replying in Finnish.

"Oh-kay."

I had no clue what he was getting at and didn't care. Tate won the face-off and shuttled the puck to me. I juked around Lankinen and his soup discussion. A lane opened in front of me, one of a few gaps that had appeared in the Finns' coverage. I skated hard toward the net, turning at the last second, puck on my stick. The Finnish goalie went down on one knee as I sailed toward him. I shoved the puck between his legs right before he closed down his five hole. Hoping to see the puck cross the line, I was knocked into the net. I threw my arms up to shield my face as a mountain of players fell on me. My shoulder slammed into the pipe. Someone slid under me. A helmet skittered across the ice. A blue one. The mass of bodies pushed forward, shoving the net off its moorings. The Finnish goalie started shouting as men began throwing punches.

I glanced down and saw Aarni lying deadly still under the mass of players, his cheek resting on the ice, his helmet several feet away. I shoved at the guy on my back, breaking out of the angry mob. I bent over Aarni, protecting him as best as I could from the fights taking place around us. Braced over the unconscious Lankinen, I began yelling for a trainer. My shouts fell on deaf ears for a second or two until the Finnish goalie noticed me caged over Aarni. Then he shouted for help. Things quieted then. I got to my skates only when the head trainer for Team Finland arrived. Lankinen had still not moved. I glanced back at my team, and it was then that I saw that the red light behind the net was still flashing. I'd scored.

Somehow that goal seemed insignificant now.

We went on to win by that single goal, but it felt hollow. The Finns had wilted after they'd stretchered Lankinen off the ice, which I totally got. Advancing was great, sure, but not at the expense of another player, even if that player was Aarni Lankinen.

I texted Jared after the game—seated in the locker room, coated with sweat and stink and sadness. My husband was happy for us, obviously, but I was having trouble working up any real joy.

J- You seem quiet. Anything I can do to help?

I gazed at the text from Jared. He knew me so well that he could pick up from a text that I was down. Fuck, but I loved him.

T-Yeah. I have to visit Aarni.

A pause as huge as a pregnant elephant. I waited for him to ask me why, and I wasn't sure I even had an answer to that—it was an instinctive need to check on him. Or something darker? Whatever it was, I needed to do it.

J-Are you sure?

T-Totally sure.

Another pause.

J-Okay. I'll see what I can find out.

T-I love you.

J-Love you too. Will let you know what I find out.

An hour and a half later, my rather silent husband and I were on our way to the China-Japan Friendship Hospital.

Chapter Eleven

Jared

I'd pulled in a favor that meant we got to enter the hospital from a staff entrance, in the hope that no one would see us visiting Aarni. Maybe, if no one spotted us, then I could pretend it wasn't happening. Last anyone was told was that Aarni was still unconscious, and what in hell did Ten think was going to happen when he stared down at Aarni in his bed?

"Hey." I stopped in my tracks at the familiar voice, and Ten and I turned in tandem to see Bryan standing under a tree, his hands in the pockets of his voluminous Team Canada coat. I faltered, not knowing what to say to the young goalie who'd been another of Aarni's victims, but in a different way. Abuse was the single word that summed up what Aarni had done to Bryan, and then to others. Hell, stories were coming out of the woodwork, some the public would never know. The latest connected to Xander Holden out of the Boston Rebels—his partner Mason had revealed to Ten that Aarni had cornered him a long time ago, and it just fueled my assumption that Aarni couldn't be redeemed —he'd been an asshole for way longer than we'd known him.

When I stopped, Ten immediately crossed to Bryan and did this complicated fist-bump thing, followed by a bro-hug. They might have been rivals here, but Bryan was the Railers' backup goalie, and he and Ten were friends first, rivals second.

They held a murmured conversation, both glancing at me, but I stopped myself from getting involved in whatever thoughts they might be sharing. Ten would call me over if he needed me—and I had to trust that I would be his first thought if he wanted help. It didn't surprise me when Bryan walked toward me at Ten's side. What reason would Bryan have for lurking here other than knowing that Ten would want to visit with Aarni.

"What you did was a brave thing," Bryan said in the softest tone, "I don't think I would have tried to protect him."

Ten side-hugged him. "Yeah, you would. You don't have an ounce of hate in you, and you'd want to keep anyone safe."

"That's what Gatlin says, but…" they ended up next to me, and Bryan and I exchanged nods. "… sometimes I have really dark thoughts."

The security guard checked his tablet and our IDs, and after a few minutes of waiting, Bryan was cleared as well, and all three of us went in. There were protocols, levels of security to even get through the next door, but Lars Johansson, a Swedish speed skater with his right leg in plaster, was a diversion as he explained how he'd hit the barrier at a million miles an hour.

It was gallows humor for a sportsman to laugh off injury, but we all pretended to ignore the devastation in his expression that his medaling chance was gone. One slip of a blade and that could have been anyone slamming into a barrier, or sliding into a wall, and a familiar tension gripped me. I tried not to dwell on the time Ten had been in the hospital, but just the scent of this place, the hushed talking, the squeak of shoes on the vinyl, and the air of fear, was enough to have my stomach rolling. I guess some of that must have shown in my expression, because Ten took my hand and laced our fingers.

We were finally let through, and it struck me as we hovered by the desk, that I didn't know what we were going to do, even though we were here. What did Ten want from this? Or Bryan? What did they think they were going to achieve—was it some weird need to see the man broken in his bed? Was it a twisted thing I couldn't comprehend? Or was it just compassion originating from who knows where?

The photos of Ten and Aarni shaking hands at the beginning of the game had gone out to the world, along with the ones of Ten literally using his own body to cradle the space around Aarni's head. Ten was a goddamn hero— a true skater with a heart of gold, someone who cared about his fellow man.

Aarni? He was just… a fucking bastard asshole who I would've rather punched than look at.

There. I was being honest with myself, and it didn't

matter that Ten had a hold of my hand; my black heart was telling my brain that I was pleased Aarni had gotten hurt.

And what did that say about me? I'm not that guy. I'm the super polite Canadian who loved his family, had a wonderful friendship with an ex-wife, had the perfect son, and was married—happily—to the man of my freaking dreams. I was happy-Jared, contented-Jared. I was certainly not homicidal-raging-Jared.

The team liaison approached us after yet another thirty-minute wait in which I stripped down my emotions and tore the painful ones apart until they were nothing but dust. If Ten wanted to be the better man, then I could follow his lead.

"Coach Madsen," the young woman said and extended her hand.

I shook it. "Madsen-Rowe, call me Jared. This is my husband Ten, and our friend, Bryan."

After the introductions were done, she pulled us into a side room, and made us coffee—as if I needed another reason not to sleep tonight. At least tomorrow was a rest day, if you call resting a practice skate and me angsting over the defense lines for our next game against who the hell knows. It all depended on the skate-offs. Hell, it could be the USA.

I will not think about things that haven't happened yet.

"So, Mr. Lankinen is awake and in stable condition. In line with the advice the doctor is giving, and with the protocols in place where family isn't available, it's very unlikely that you'll be able to visit face-to-face with Mr. Lankinen at present."

Ten frowned, and I jumped in. "I was led to believe that he would be allowed visitors."

"Visitors that he will allow, certainly."

"Okay." I was so fucking relieved that it must have shown because Ten's frown deepened. I wanted to fix things, but Aarni wouldn't let Ten and Bryan anywhere near him—what sane man would want his past revisited on him in a closed space. He'd already faced sanctions and a case for a car accident he'd caused, and how he'd escaped any of that without a criminal record astounded me. Maybe his time would come, maybe he'd step over the line, but if they were seeking any form of understanding from Aarni, then it was a futile objective. They were mistaken if they thought Aarni would be interested in listening to them— he'd more likely try to justify his position and inflict more psychological damage.

"Would you ask him for us?" Ten pointed at his chest, "Tennant Madsen-Rowe and Bryan Delaney."

She dutifully scribbled the names on a pad and then headed down a long hallway and through a door marked *private*.

"What are you even trying to achieve here?" I blurted, all my silent support at arranging this slipping away as the reality of being there hit me.

Ten and Bryan exchanged glances.

"I need to see him hurt," Bryan began miserably, then shook his head. "Before you say it, I know that makes me a shit person, but I need to go in there…" he pulled back his shoulders, "… and I need to know that when he's down, I'm the bigger man, and I can show compassion, and I can shake all the final, terrifying ghosts free."

As soon as he finished, his eyes widened as if he'd never expected those words to leave his mouth.

Ten huffed, then nodded. "Same really," he said with so much honesty I wanted to hold him close and never let him go.

Footsteps alerted us to the liaison coming back, her ponytail swinging as she came toward us.

"He'll see you. " She sounded surprised; but hell, she wasn't as surprised as me. "You understand that I won't leave the room." She waited for Ten and Bryan to nod. "If you want to come with me."

I fixed my gaze on the Finland flag on her shirt because this was nothing like what I wanted to happen, but I had to stay quiet. Bryan went with her to the door, Ten squeezing my hand then following, and all I could do was slump to the nearest chair and not look as if the worries of the world had suddenly landed on my shoulders.

My cell vibrated, and I was thankful for the interruption—it was Oli and he cut straight to the chase.

"Di Costa pulled a fucking muscle and kept it a big fucking secret, fucking goalies. He's getting physio now, but that means we have no choice but to start Bryan Delaney in the next game."

"That's not a bad thing," I reassured him. The fact Bryan was here at the hospital showed a maturity beyond his years—at least I think that is what it meant.

"No, Bryan's good, and there's a reason he's here. He's a great goalie, so much potential if he keeps his head in the game, but if we're facing Germany, or Sweden, then, they're a physical team, and I worry they'll intimidate him."

"He's stronger than you think." I glanced at the door, but there was nothing.

"I know," Oli said with another sigh. "It's not even that. I'm just pissed at Di Costa."

I lowered my voice—given anyone could be listening. "I guess we need to cover which D-men will work best with him, just in case?"

Oli looked relieved. "Please."

"I'll be back soon." I ended the call and focused back on that damn door, back to the weirdest night of my life.

Weirder even than when Stan had made us dress up as cats for Noah's birthday party.

And that was *weird*.

Chapter Twelve

Ten

It was more than surreal stepping into that room—the smells, the sounds, the hushed whispers of the nurse on duty as she moved around Aarni, checking his vitals. It brought back my time in the hospital with such force I had to latch onto a chair to keep from buckling.

All those days, weeks, months spent in rehab, the fear I might never play again, the realization that, while I was ninety-five percent healed, my brain would never be as it had been. The lingering side effects... the brain fog, the migraines, the gaps that would pop up out of nowhere. The recollection of my mother's prayers, my father's grim face, my brothers' pacing, my husband's tears when he thought I was sleeping...

All that pain and suffering because of this human being.

Fingers biting into the chair frame, I had to tamp down the urge to bray at his misfortune. As I breathed in the smell of disinfectant, a battle waged on inside me. It was human nature, I guess, that desire to laugh at those who have caused you pain when they're felled. Kick them when they're down and all that. Bryan stood at my side, face locked into some cold-ass mask, like an automaton bereft of all feeling. What was he thinking? Was he laughing inside? Raging? Weeping? Whatever he was experiencing, he was locking that shit down tight.

"Five minutes," the nurse said, then moved to the corner of the room to tap away on a laptop.

Aarni looked our way, his face showing recognition. I wet my lips as my throat was suddenly dry as the Sahara.

"Thanks for agreeing to see us," I opened with. Bryan tensed at my side, his lips pressed into a papercut thin line. "I'm glad your injury wasn't too bad. I hope that you recover quickly and can return to the ice."

He gave me a blank stare, then his gaze darted to Bryan. Machines beeped, the nurse klick-klacked on her keyboard, and out in the hallway someone rushed by.

"Bryan," Aarni stared at him, and then at me, and I swear even in pain, he sneered at me, and then returned to stare back at Bryan with a confident expression. I was ready to step in to block Aarni's view of Bryan—or maybe Bryan's of Aarni.

"Thank you for protecting my head," Aarni forced out even as he couldn't take his eyes off of Bryan.

"I'd do the same for any man down on the ice," I replied, and got nothing in return from him.

"I owe you thanks, but I have nothing else for you if you're expecting some great emotional speech." He looked so pale. "So is that it?" he asked, and even in pain he was tense. I guess he was expecting either Bryan or I to have a lot more to say. He turned his head to Bryan. "I guess you won't have the guts to say anything at all."

"Fuck you." Bryan said evenly. "I've seen what I needed to see." I was surprised to see a soft smile on his face where there should have been anger.

"What about you, Rowe?" he glanced at me, and there was no emotion in his eyes. He didn't care about us—I imagine he didn't even care I saved his life. What kind of headspace was he in right now to have the man he'd nearly killed turning around and keeping him safe?

"Madsen-Rowe," I corrected gently.

"Whatever." He looked over at the nurse. "I'm tired. Send them away please," he croaked, then closed his eyes. I heard Bryan pull in a sharp breath right before he spun and left the room.

"I'll let myself out," I said as the nurse glanced at me in that firm way medical professionals have when they're protecting their patient. I respected that. She didn't know what a slug Aarni was. All she knew was that he was hurt, and it was her job to tend to him. That was noble as hell. I glanced at Aarni as I tried to think of what to say as I left. *Goodbye* seemed lacking. *Fuck all the way off, you miserable asshole* felt right, but that wasn't at all what my mother would wish for me to say.

I settled on leaving. Obviously, I had said all I had wanted to say to Aarni. I'd been the bigger man, acted with the honor that the Rowe name demanded. Stepping out into the brightly lit corridor, I sucked in a shaky breath, my fingers coming up to rest on the lion prancing on my throat. I could feel the scar that was hidden there under the brilliant inkwork—the raised flesh where that skate blade had come within millimeters of severing my jugular. My fingertips traced the bumpy skin as my heartrate dropped. I'd not even been aware of how jazzed my nervous system had been during that visit. I blew out a breath, lowered my hand, and went to find Bryan and Jared. They were easy to locate. Jared was in a small waiting area trying to get Bryan to take a cup of coffee.

"Hey," I said softly, easing into the cramped room filled with people awaiting news of loved ones. Several pairs of eyes lifted. I smiled at the people staring at me, at *us*, as if we were from another planet. We did tend to outsize most of the people in Beijing, and our Team USA and Team Canada gear helped to stick out even more than we normally would. "I'll take that." Jared studied me with concern as he passed over the coffee. Nope, tea, it was tea. The smell was pleasant and sweet. "Let's go. You want to go?"

"Yes please," Bryan replied, tension radiating from him.

Jared opened his mouth, but I shook my head. This wasn't the place. The press were around I was sure. They followed us everywhere we went. Jared and I followed Bryan. My husband's worry was palpable. I gave Jared a wobbly smile or two, sipped the hot tea, and felt a shudder move over me as we found ourselves in the lobby, the cold air blowing in every time the sliding doors opened and shut.

"Hey, man, you good?" I asked of my teammate and friend.

Bryan blew out a long breath, then slowly nodded.

"Yeah. Mostly. No? I don't know." He shrugged, his face twisted in confusion. "Maybe. Yeah, I'm okay. I just need to parse it all out and talk to Gatlin." His gaze dropped from the ceiling to Jared, then moved to me. "Thanks for letting me come along. I think it helped."

Bryan held out a fist to Jared, and they bumped immediately. "Later, Coach," he murmured, and then headed out the way we'd come in.

"Okay?" Jared asked as soon as we were alone, but I shook my head. *Not here.*

All too soon, we were back in the cold air, fingers laced, and I knew Jared was worried I was so quiet.

He filled the silence. "What do you think of Germany beating Slovakia? It was close. Germany was on fire, but their goalie was slow on that last goal. I really thought Slovakia might pull it off, but I guess with Germany being one of the favorites, it was always going to be hard for Slovakia to get that miracle. Hey, I guess that means there's still a miracle out there waiting to be found? Maybe one of us will get it, and end up with the gold—"

I stopped him talking with a quick kiss.

"It's okay."

"It's not."

I waited a beat. "It will be."

Our ride turned up, and before we could talk more, we were heading back to the Olympic Village, flashing our passes, and ending up outside the Team Canada building. Team USA was a short walk from there, and I needed the air just as much as I needed not to leave Jared right now, so we paid and then stood in the shadows cast by a huge advertising awning.

"Can you tell me?" Jared asked.

"He seemed strong, a concussion, but no cracks or anything worse. He just looked at us, vacantly, as if we were nothing to him. It was chilling." I paused for a moment and stared off into the middle distance before continuing. "Bryan didn't say anything to him, and I just told Aarni that I hoped he was okay and that if there was anything I could do. He thanked me for protecting his head, but it was in this dead tone, as if there was nothing in his life experience that had taught him how to handle someone's compassion. I mean, do you think something is broken inside of him? Or maybe he wasn't loved as a child, or… I don't know. I just don't understand it."

"Maybe there is nothing to understand," Jared murmured and hugged me again. I wanted to stay in his arms, but anyone could walk past, and I wasn't in the right headspace to deal with any shit right now.

"I'm a little concerned about Germany," I changed the subject. "But if we're not going up against you guys again, then knowing our luck, we'll be matched to Russia, and I'll be facing Stan in net."

"Much small net with big pipes," Jared tried for my Stan-accent, something he had been practicing since his and Stan's road trip, and I couldn't help snorting a laugh. Then we kissed briefly—discreetly—and I stepped away. "I love you."

"Not as much as I love you."

Chapter Thirteen

Ten

Two days later, I was sitting beside a lotus pond outside the Summer Palace in Lianhuachi Park. The air was brisk. My travelling partner aka roommate was seated beside me on a bench as we wasted a few hours between a brutal morning skate and our game against Russia this evening. He was also busking. An arrest was imminent.

"… summer this pond is covered with lotus blossoms that fill the air with a heady, sweet fragrance. Doū Xiè." A passing Chinese couple dropped some coins into his goalie helmet as he strummed an old Cat Stevens song on his beloved acoustic guitar. I knew I should have gone with Tate and the others to see the Forbidden City, but Colorado had been set on Lotus Park, and I didn't want him to be alone. Jared was right. Sometimes, I was too nice for my own good. "It used to be a summer residence for the royal families. Can you imagine waking up and stepping out to breathe the glorious scent of lotus on the air?" He inhaled as if he could pick up the scent.

I glanced over my shoulder nervously. Any second now someone in the dark green of the Beijing police would swoop down upon us. We'd be in jail. Forever. I'd never see Lottie grow up and my dog would die. We didn't have a dog, but I wanted one, and it would be dead before I'd ever see the light of day again. Fuck. I was spiraling.

"Why are you asking for money?" I blurted out. Colorado chuckled softly. "What? I mean if you need cash for soda or guitar picks—"

"I'm not asking for myself. I'm flush, but thanks. I'm collecting for the park itself. See that note taped to the cage of my mask?" I did, but it was in Chinese. "That says all funds collected will be donated to the park itself. It's all good."

I was beginning to suspect him whenever he said that. "How do you know how to speak and write Mandarin so well?"

"I have a sharp brain." He tossed his hair from his face and gave me a wink. "So, tell me how the trip to see Lankinen went."

"I told you already. Is that a cop?"

"Nah, I mean tell me what you've come away with from going to see him." He moved from Cat Stevens to an old Rolling Stones classic about wild horses. Jared loved that one. "What led you to go see him? For what cause?"

"Oh." I looked out over the pond, suddenly wishing that it was summer so that the flowers would be in bloom. I bet it was gorgeous. "I think I wanted to offer him an olive branch, you know? I wanted to see if I could settle things between us. Let him know that I knew what he was going through."

"That's righteous." He nodded at a French couple. "Merci bien," he called to the tourists.

"How many languages do you speak?"

"Oh, well, with the addition of Mandarin, about eight? I never knew I was so attuned to languages, then we bought a tape for Madeline so she could learn Welsh. Joe has some Welsh blood in his family, and I thought a multilingual kid would be cool. The words just kind of downloaded into my head. Kind of like song lyrics and hockey plays. I'm going to learn Russian next. This way I can razz Vlad in his native tongue. He'll fucking hate that." He sniggered mischievously. "So back to Aarni. Were you pissed when he blew you off?"

"Maybe, a little, but… sure, I guess." I shoved my hands into the pockets of my Team USA jacket. The surface of the pond rippled in the wind. "I mean sure I was hurt. I made this effort to be forgiving, and he spit in my eye."

"We have no control over others."

"And the way he stared at Bryan—like he wanted to intimidate him." I shuddered at the memory. There was so much hate in that man, and certainly no redemption. Bryan had been so brave standing there and facing that sadistic hate.

"I know, and now that I went and saw him, gave him the chance to be a decent human being, and he turned from that open hand of friendship, I can write him off. The closure feels good. Forgiveness creates peace."

"It looks good on you." I threw him a shy smile. He

grinned back. "Right, well my stomach is telling me it's time for some protein. Also that cop over there is giving us the stink eye."

I reacted like my head was on a swivel. *"Where's a cop?!"*

"I'm shitting you dude, there's no cop." He slapped me hard on the back. "You're so tight. Maybe we should find a massage parlor after we eat."

"Jared would *not* be cool with that."

"I know, I'm just busting your balls."

"I really fucking hate you," I mumbled, then nudged him in the side. He snorted.

Goalies were *so* damned weird.

I felt his gray eyes on me during warmup. Knowing that I'd not have much time to speak to my best friend before the game started, I skated slowly over to where he and another Russian goalie were doing their stretches. Just watching the splits and backbends taking place made my hamstrings ache. Stan glanced up, his expression one of cool detachment, but I knew better. Deep down, I saw that spark that said, "Here is my bestie in whole world!"

We'd met up a few times here and there over the past week, but relations with ROC and most of the other teams was tense. And knowing how the Russian government disliked Stan and all he stood for—an out gay man married to another man, as well as a proud new American citizen— we'd agreed beforehand to be cool in public. People knew we were both Railers, so that afforded us some leeway, but we'd just basically nod or lift a hand in greeting as we passed. I had no wish to bring any kind of upset on Stan or his family. He may be an American with dual citizenship now, but he had relatives in Russia. It was sad that we had to walk such a delicate line with international relationships, but there it was. I'd sooner have cut off my arm than bring any harm to anyone Stan was close to.

"Hey there," I said as I scanned the crowds piling into the rink. "I hear your pipes have been really nice to you."

"Yes, they have been most kind." He rose slowly, his intimidating height made even more imposing with him in skates. He looked as wide as he was tall. "You do realize that they sing a song of silent electric boogaloo to me. The only songs *you* will hear is the pained squeal of your shots hitting iron or the inside of my mitt."

I had to smile. He was talking true shit, but there was a glimmer of the imp in his gaze.

"We'll see about that. I've got some moves that you might not have seen before."

"That is doubtful." He smiled softly, patted my head as if I were a puppy, and skated off to whisper sweet nothings to his pipes. The other goalie, a young kid named Arytom Sidorov from the LA team nodded. He spoke little English. His glove hand was insane. Not as good as Stan's, and he lacked the experience that Stan had.

"You stirring up the pot?" our team captain asked when I made a lazy lap to catch up to him.

"*Me?*" I asked with the utmost sincerity.

Tate snorted.

About thirty minutes later, the quarterfinal showdown between USA and ROC began.

Things were a little odd to start, both teams seemingly

feeling each other out. Colorado fielded a few loopy shots, as did Stan. We all knew this would not be one of the crazy blowouts like we'd seen between Denmark and Sweden. This would be a goalie showdown with lots of heavy hitting. Tate got that first slam to the boards about forty-five seconds after the start of the game. Vlad drove his shoulder into him, the impact making me wince when the captain of the US team crashed off the glass. No one could ever accuse Vlad of playing favorites with his lover, Tate. The puck was picked up by a Russian forward. Vlad looked across the ice, finding me just over Stan's left shoulder. He pointed at me. A clear, You're-next-puny-American move right out of Ivan Drago's playbook.

"Okay, fucker," I snarled, lowered my head, and chased the man with the puck. I caught up to him with ease, stole the rubber disc, and then executed a tight drop pass to Tate who'd picked himself up. We raced back to the ROC net, passing crisply between us. Stan was low on his skates, his big body leaving little room to go high, and his pads already dropping to bar any shots from slipping through the wickets. Tate took a shot. It went wide and high, cracking off a stanchion to bounce into the netting. Whistles blew. I sailed past Novikov blithely. "Iceberg is right. You're slow as one," I said as I cruised past Vlad.

His reply was something in Russian that made Stan glance back at us. That set the tone for the rest of the game. Hardnosed hockey was being doled out all over the ice. When we did get a breakaway or a sleek shot attempt, Stan shut us down. Colorado was a wall of ice in our net, moving with grace and ease from side to side, blades on the pipes, catching mitt a blur. Both netminders were putting on a show. The rest of us were too busy trying to stay on our skates while checking, blocking shots, and shoving our faces into opposing players gloves. Oh wait, that might just have been me. Vlad had put a target on my back, and every damn time I was on the ice, there he was,, —poking, prodding, rubbing his glove across my nose, or knocking me ass over tin cups.

The final straw came late in the third period with two fat goose eggs on the scoreboard. I also had a knot on my head, but that was inconsequential. Jared would fret. I was fine. Just tired of being used for a punching bag. I came a little unglued on the defensemen during a TV time out. I even threw a glove. Which was totally unlike me, but for fucking fuck's sake, someone had to put an end to the Iceberg or Team US of A was going to sink. With four minutes left, I thundered out to take a face-off, leaving my teammates with hangdog looks. Which made me feel bad. I'd apologize later—if I could lift myself out of the ice bath I was going to have to take. My bruises had bruises.

Tate picked up the puck behind our net, carrying it out to the blue line where he passed it to me. It was a little weak. I let the puck bounce off my back skate, never breaking stride, shunting it forward to my stick. Tate skated into the ROC zone at Mach speed. I shot it back to him, the reception beautiful on his end. Stan's gaze darted from me to Tate a second too late. Tate's shot was like a bullet out of a rifle. Stan threw up the glove, but it was a millisecond behind the puck slapping into the net. The twine shook. Tate and I threw our arms around each other on the left-hand side of the ROC goal, the others on our line slamming into us to shout and pat our helmets. I was thrilled to get the assist. The captain got the game winning goal, and Colorado shut down the opposing team neatly. Like shut-the-door-and-lock-it-no-one-was-getting-in-past-Colorado. The buzzer sounded after a hair-raising final minute and twenty seconds with an extra skater on for ROC. Stan was on the bench cursing violently, his pewter eyes like a raging hurricane. My best friend did not take losing well.

He'd calm down soon. When we gathered on the ice for the handshake—now a fist-bump—line, Stan's gaze was still fiery, but his smile was genuine.

"Next time in practice, I will shut you down so hard your name will be Billy Brick," he said, ruffling my sweaty hair with his blocker.

"I look forward to it. Love 'ya, man." I tapped his chest, then moved on, basking in the glory of a hard-won victory. I basked for about five minutes, which wasn't nearly enough time. Coach rounded us all up in the dressing room with a sharp whistle. The joking and back-slapping quieted.

"Well-played game," he said with a smile that finally reached his eyes. "Enjoy your celly. Tomorrow, we start training twice as hard. Canada just beat Germany over in the other barn."

Well shit. I glanced at my skates. Looked like it was going to be us against Jared in the semi-final round. I'd better double up on the ibuprofen intake and whisper a prayer to the hockey gods for guidance and protection. If we had thought the Russian defense was brutal, wait until we had to face the pairings my husband was going to fire at us.

Maybe I'd better triple-up my ibuprofen consumption. And eat lots of Wheaties.

Chapter Fourteen

Jared

Team USA beat Russia, Sweden took Denmark to the wire and managed a win, Switzerland left no space for the Czech team to get going. That left Canada facing the US in the semis, and Sweden facing Switzerland.

Last four teams standing.

There was an inevitability about us going up against Team USA again—almost as if fate had already decided one of us would go home with gold. Of course, we'd have to beat whichever of Sweden or Switzerland got into the final, but I had a strong feeling that it was Canada or the US who would be heading for Olympic gold. But the strangeness I felt was mixed with seeing Stan after his game, seeing his devastation and disappointment that he couldn't carry ROC to the final, and understanding how he felt.

Our game against the US was today, and right now I

needed to see Ryker. I knocked on his door, and a perky Sawyer answered, then stepped back and let me in.

"Ryker, your dad's here, uhm… Coach Madsen-Rowe is here." I could hear the shower, and wondered if he'd heard, but I'd sit and wait. Sawyer grabbed his jacket. "Coffee run, you want something, Coach?"

"I'm good."

"Okay then, back in ten."

Sawyer left before I could ask him anything about Aarni, or about his feelings, which was probably a good thing given how close I was to the situation. I wasn't saying I truly believed Ten had forgiven Aarni completely, but he'd said he had, and he'd found a certain peace, and I had to assume that Bryan was in the same place. I shut the door behind him and sat on Ryker's bed—it was easy to tell which one was his. Sawyer's side of the room was immaculate, everything neat as a pin. Ryker had clearly held on to his teenage years, with a tumble of personal items on the cabinet by his bed—photos, phone chargers, his iPad, a Kindle, one screwed up Canada tee. I sat on my hands as long as I could, and then tidied the pile, making sure his phone was charging, then stood the photos up along the wall.

There was a picture of him and Jacob taken at their ranch, an Arizona sunset casting a glow about them as they grinned into the camera. I loved Jacob—strong, steady and so completely in love with my son—and for a moment my thoughts wandered back to the gorgeous wedding they'd had, and the love that seemed to filter out from the photo. Then there was a picture of Ryker holding Lottie, beaming down at her, so happy to have a new sister, and another photo of him with his other sisters—Sophia, Ava, and Lilly —his arms around them all, his mom behind them, pulling them into a hug. Finally, there was one of the three of us— me, Ryker, and Ten—us in our red and white, and Ten in the middle sporting the US colors, with his hands over the maple leaves on our shirts.

I remembered that day so well, celebrating Ten and Ryker getting spots on their respective Olympic teams and me as the Canadian defensive coach—we had so much to be happy for.

"They're a strong team," Ryker murmured, and I realized he'd come out of the bathroom, in team sweats, his hair wrapped in a towel, and was sitting on Sawyer's crisply made bed. How hadn't I heard him? "The US, I mean—they're strong."

"They are—watch out for Dominguez, he pushes and—"

"Dad, are you okay?"

I sighed and placed the photo back on the cabinet, sliding it along until all four photos were in a row.

"Sure," I lied.

"Oh shit, that is your weird face."

"My what now?"

"The one you get when all your worries collide, and you don't know what to handle first, and they all end up making you do the weird face thing."

"I have a perfectly fine face."

"Apart from when it's all screwed up." He pulled an expression that I assume was to show me what I looked like. It wasn't attractive. "So, is it a coach worry, a country rivals concern, a Lottie thing, or a Ten thing?"

I huffed a laugh at the direct questions. "No, it's a Ryker thing."

"Oh." He didn't know how to answer that and focused on gently patting his hair. His curls had always been the bane of his life, but he had it down as to how to deal with them. I noticed he'd let them grow long enough to tie back in games, and it reminded me of the time he'd decided he hated his curly hair and had shaved half of it off. He'd been ten or so, and said he'd done it just because it was getting in the way of him playing hockey. I'd understood where he was coming from—after all, hockey had been everything to me as well—case in point, my short relationship with his mom.

"I'm so proud of you, Ryker."

He wrinkled his nose. "I'm proud of you, too. You're the best defensive coach that—"

"No, I'm not proud of you for getting chosen—I mean, of course I'm proud." I wasn't making sense, and I scrubbed at my eyes briefly. "I'm proud of the man you are now. For the work you do on and off the ice, for how you love Jacob so much, for how good you are with your sisters—all four of your sisters—and for how much you're changing the world for good."

He stopped patting at his hair and folded the towel in his lap, as if he needed time to think. "Thanks," he said after a long pause. "Dad? Are you okay? Is it Ten? Is it the Aarni thing? Are you going to cry? Shit, Dad, what's wrong?"

I blinked away the emotion. "I'm not going to cry—"

"It's okay if you need to. You know I won't judge you. I might tease you, but if you need to cry then—"

"Ry, I'm okay. I just needed you to know that whatever happens today, win or lose, I'm so damn proud of you for everything."

"Oh." He moved then, came to sit next to me, our shoulders touching. "It's not a Ryker-thing, it's a Ryker-playing-hockey thing."

"Yeah."

"What is worrying you specifically?"

"That we go out there, lose to the USA, and you don't get gold, and I want that for you, and I also want it for Ten, and—"

Ryker bumped my shoulder to stop me talking. "Do you remember that game against the Tremblay Hogs when I was twelve? The summer charity thing back home?"

I remembered it clearly because it was only one of the times I nearly lost my shit at a kids hockey game. I'd still been playing professionally then, but Luca Tremblay, local business owner, had been a wannabe player who took his frustrations out on the kids he'd corralled onto his team. "Sure, I do."

"But do you remember that you wanted to kill Tremblay after that game. Hell, I'm surprised you didn't slide over the entire rink and punch that asshole out."

"I nearly did. Hell, it was a kids' charity match, and he took it too seriously. Asshole was pushing his team too hard, made a couple of them cry."

"See, that's it right there."

"What?" Now, I really was confused, but knowing my

son, he had something profound he was trying to say—he was so much like his mom sometimes with his insightful comments.

"You just want everyone to be able to play hockey—cleanly, fairly, and the lesson is that there will be wins, and losses, and that's okay."

"Oh."

"You didn't punch him. That took restraint, but mostly, you went over there, and you calmed everyone down, and you made it fun again for those kids. It's what you taught me, too. I know that hockey isn't just a game. I play to get a salary. It's in my bones, it's part of me, and I love it; and that's because you helped me see that when I play with my heart, win or lose the game, I'm the best man I can be."

"Oh," I repeated.

"Also, I saw you trip him up on the bench when no one else was looking. So… go Dad!"

I blinked at my son, saw the start of a smirk, and then I couldn't help smirking back and then laughing. When he joined in, we hugged and laughed, and all the worries I had about USA versus Canada slipped away. I couldn't stop laughing; he couldn't either. Not even Sawyer coming back into the room was enough for the father-son bonding moment to end.

Exactly as it should be.

The game was anticlimactic after all my worries.

It was obvious that the US had the measure of us from the moment the puck dropped. It didn't matter who I sent out against Ten, there was always Tate on the next line.

Defend against Tate, then there was Ten waiting in the wings. Throw in a penalty against us that we should never have let happen, Ten and Tate both on the power play, and there was no way we could stop the goal Ten scored against Bryan. By the time the first period was done—a scrappy fractious twenty minutes where we seemed to make too many mistakes and had zero on the board—Team USA had one.

We'd started Bryan because Di Costa wasn't a hundred percent, and while Bryan was an amazing backup, he wasn't able to lead from behind in the same way that Di Costa would have done. I could see the frustration in Bryan, as the defense weren't exactly doing their bit to keep his net clear. There was nothing specifically wrong with any part of our team; they just weren't gelling, and the US was dominating.

Period two was better, after a talk from Coach that consisted of stony-eyed glares and a threat he'd leave us all in China. But not even the threat was going to pull the team out of the slowly widening pit, and even though everything was tighter in the second period, there wasn't enough we could do.

Ten was on fire, and so damn fast, and wily, and just about every other amazing adjective I could think of where hockey was concerned. He and Tate were gold medal skaters, and they were putting on a show.

When Ryker got caught for a penalty, skating angrily to the box, it was inevitable that, with a man down, we couldn't stop the US; and when Tate and Ten went over the boards on the powerplay, I knew they'd score.

Seventeen seconds was all it took.

First a face-off, which Tate won, shuttling the puck to Ten, who miraculously evaded anyone in the red and white and passed it back to Tate, who was clear of anyone who could stop him. Ten was *right there*, open when Tate took a shot and it rebounded. He collected it, so close to Bryan's glove that, for a second, I couldn't tell if Bryan had caught the puck.

But the roar of the US fans, the light, and the celebration, and it was two for the US, and Canada with a big fat zero.

The pep talk between periods two and three was even stonier, but Coach at least pulled out some positives, and even though I wanted to go over and reassure Ryker, that wasn't my job, and I had to fight not to go into dad-mode.

The third period was war, every lesson we'd learned going up against the Ten/Tate duo was used, but we couldn't get the commitment to work for a goal, and when the final buzzer sounded, we'd lost three-zero, and it was a despondent Canada that slogged into the changing rooms.

"We never stood a chance," someone muttered.

They were kind of right.

We'd meet Switzerland in the play-off for the bronze. The US would play Sweden for the gold.

It was a sad moment for us, and we owned that disappointment as a team, but we couldn't lose hope. A bronze medal at the winter Olympics was something rare and precious, and yeah, it might not be gold, but it was a win on an international stage that should make us proud.

I managed to fist-bump Ryker, imbuing that soft touch with as much fatherly love as I could, and he raised an eyebrow.

"Go Ten," he murmured so no one else would hear, and added a smile.

Pride mixed with sadness that was all wound up with love.

"Him and Tate…" I whispered back.

"Yeah… unstoppable."

Chapter Fifteen

Ien

After you're married for a bit, you get to know your spouse well.

Which was how I knew that Jared would be in a pretty vulnerable place after our game. It was an odd situation for us. We always shared our team victories—and losses—together. Our emotions ran on similar paths as we were both on the same team. But this was new. I wasn't sure I liked it, and I was really sure I had no clear way to handle it. All the texts from family, friends, and teammates back home ran along the same path:

Congrats! No small feat beating Canada! How's Jared and Ryker?

. . .

After a shower and some press time, I'd fired off several texts to my husband. He'd replied with all kinds of affirmations that he was proud and happy for me. And he was, but there was a vibe to his replies that I sensed meant that he needed more than some text messages. I tossed my phone to the nightstand then got off my hard-as-marble slab bed to knock on the bathroom door.

A naked Colorado opened it, his hair piled on top of his head in this crazy Pebbles Flintstone sort of style, his junk hanging in the breeze.

"Dude, seriously, cover your tackle." I closed my eyes.

He snorted in amusement. "Did you try out the bidet yet?" he asked. I peeked to see if he had covered his balls. He had. Sort of. With a damp towel held over his crotch. "I mean holy fucking wow! Why are they not more popular in the States? I'm totally doing a shitter overhaul when I get home. Bidets all the way! The showers here are for shit, but the crappers? Fucking bestial."

He did have a point about the showers here. I could barely squeeze myself into the narrow stalls. The toilets? I'd not really paid all that much mind, but sure, a bidet was nice.

"Can I ask you a huge favor?" I enquired.

"You want to invite the hubby over for some hugging, kissing, and squeezing time?"

"He's kind of down."

"Yeah, that was for sure a rough one for them. Yeah, invite him over. I'll go grab some clothes and sleep on Tate's floor. He misses me."

I wasn't sure that the team captain missed him all that much, but I thanked him just the same. I'd deal with Tate in the morning. As soon as Colorado was gone, I sent Jared a quick invite. He'd just left Ryker's room it seemed. Man, I wished I could have been there with them both.

I spent a little time in the bathroom, then padded around our room, kicking a sneaker back under Colorado's bed to join its brethren, as well as a massive stuffed Chinese dragon he'd bought for his daughter that was also wedged under there. The poor kid would probably have nightmares if it was looming over her crib, but who was I to comment?

A soft rap, about ten minutes later, had me hurrying to answer the door. Jared stood in the hallway in his red and white jacket, his smile soft, but not reaching those beautiful eyes of his. I reached out, grabbed his wrist, and tugged him into the room.

"You stand out," I whispered, sliding my hands up to his shoulders to push his jacket off his shoulders. "Some crazed US athlete will chuck a bald eagle at you. You'll retaliate with a maple syrup grenade. War between the States and Canada will erupt. International relations will fall apart. Ryan Reynolds will stop making *Deadpool* movies."

"It's that last one that you're most worried about, isn't it?" he asked as his jacket hit the floor and I stepped closer, my arms sliding around his lean middle.

"Oh totes." I buried my nose into his throat, inhaling the clean masculine scent of his warm skin mixed with aftershave.

"Also, maple syrup grenades?" He cinched me tight, his lips moving through my hair. I'd not meant for this to be as sexual as it was becoming, but hey if his dick was into it and my dick was into it—and they both were—then why not tumble into bed?

"Yeah." I nipped at his throat. A throaty purr rumbled out of him as his hands moved to my lower back. "They explode on contact, coating the victim with sticky syrup that glues them to the floor, making it easier for the Mounties to capture them."

"Mm, I see you've given this all kinds of thought. Why would Ryan Reynolds stop making *Deadpool* movies though? He could just film them in Canada."

"Stop nitpicking my scenario and kiss me."

He was all sorts of onboard for that. His mouth crashed down over mine, the kiss ravenous. His hands cupped my buttocks. My fingers clawed at his back.

"I need this," he murmured as he massaged my ass. "I need *you*."

"You got me." Mouths sealed, we kissed and tumbled to the bed, tugging at clothing as if we'd not been together in years. The fire his touch always lit in me roared to life as he yanked my zipper down, then shoved my jeans and briefs to my ankles. His hand wrapped around my cock, stroking the length, then curling over the head. He knew me so well, knew what my body needed, what it craved. "Fuck me," I gasped as he worked me.

I climbed onto the twin bed, forearms resting on the bed, ass in the air, cock throbbing. Jared made a sound of pure pleasure that went right to my balls.

"Christ that's the most beautiful sight," he growled. I smiled into my clasped hands when the sound of him rustling in my bright blue bag hit me. Eyes closed, I tried to calm my breathing. That worked for roughly seventeen seconds. Then Jared knelt on the bed. It didn't move. "What the hell do they stuff these mattresses with? Shredded concrete?"

His thighs pressed into mine, his rock-hard cock slid up the crack of my ass. He was hot as a brand and slick with lube. I groaned loudly, then shoved my face into the bedding.

"How do you want this?" he asked at the same exact time his prick breached me. I gasped, moaned, and rocked back to take more. His fingers bit into my hips. "Ah okay, it's that way then. Good." He rolled his pelvis, impaling me. Air rushed out of me, the stretch and burn a tingling brief second or two that was quickly replaced with pure pleasure. "I love how your body reacts to mine. How you pull me into you, hold me…"

"Always… always hold you when you…" His pelvis jerked. "Ah! Hell that's so good. So good, deeper, faster."

I bit down on my wrist when he gave me what I had begged for. Jared pounded me into the bedding. It was fucking glorious. He fell over me as he filled me. My knees splayed to the sides as his cock kicked and pulsed, the hot splash of his cum deep inside me giving me that little extra nudge. Hamstrings pulled tight, I arched my back, straining, head and ass rising, dick grinding into the covers. He thrust madly, his cock now bumping that bundle of nerves. I blew apart at the fourth stroke of my prostate, my cries cut off by his hand coming around to cover my mouth as he shuddered violently, his sweaty chest pressed to my back.

"Unhf," he said, then slid off and out, his cock leaving a wet trail across my ass cheek. I worked myself to the side, my hip smearing the puddle I'd made on the bed. I could not have cared less. It would wash. Jared rested on his side, facing me, his hair a mess, blue eyes glowing.

"You fucking beast," I whispered, then stole a kiss. It was a soft-as-duck-down kiss. He wiggled closer. I slid my leg between his, rested my head on my arm, and reached out to caress his beloved face. "I love you," I whispered.

"I love you more," he replied on a shaky breath. "Did I hurt you?"

"No, not at all. Well, maybe just a twinge at first, but after that? Pure fucking bliss." I traced his ear gently. The worry lines left his face. "I'm so sorry your team lost. It sucked so badly to have to play against you. I don't think I'd ever be willing to do this again."

He studied me intently. "It's all part of the game, Ten. One of us had to lose. We've been through enough playoffs and Cup finals to know that."

"Yeah, but you were at my side through all of those runs. This rivalry thing with your husband totally sucks." I ran my thumb along his jawline, lost in his eyes and the body heat he was throwing out. "This is the last time I do this."

"Don't say that. We don't know what the future holds. I might retire soon and become a fulltime stay-at-home dad to our kids." He ran a hand over my biceps, then up to my neck where he caressed the Rowe golden lion inked into my skin.

"'Kids'? Like in plural?"

"Yeah, like in plural. Siblings are amazing."

"You'd sing a different song if you had mine." That

made him chuckle. I moved closer as our skin began to cool.

"You love your brothers."

"Jamie, yeah, sometimes. Brady is a tool." He tweaked my ear. "Okay fine, I love them both. And yeah, maybe someday we can add to the family."

He stole a kiss. "That sounds wonderful." He sighed. "I suppose I should get up and get out of here before Colorado returns and gets a gander at my pale ass."

"Mm, no, he's going to sleep on Tate's floor. Stay here tonight?" I snuggled in close and kissed his scruffy chin. "We'll set an alarm so you can sneak out before dawn. Stay with me?"

"As if I could deny you anything." He tasted of my mouth for a long, sweet time. "We do need to shower though."

"And strip the cover off the bed."

"Want to shower with me?"

"I'd love to. I'm not sure we can fit, though."

"We'll wedge ourselves in."

"Cool, but let's make sure we have a phone close at hand in case we have to call maintenance to come pry us out of the stall."

He chuckled. "You're so good for me. I really needed this time with you. And I am incredibly proud. You go out there, and you win that gold medal. I'll be cheering the loudest, you know that, right?"

Yeah, I totally did.

Chapter Sixteen

Ten

It had all come down to this game.

All the flights, lost sleep, nerves, angst, worldwide attention. Everything now rested on how well twenty-five players could make hockey for three twenty-minute periods.

The morning had flown by after I'd woken to a rock star taking a shower. Nothing like a little AC/DC rolling out of the bathroom at six o'clock in the morning. I'd reached out to Jared, who was also wide awake and wide-eyed, yanking at covers to hide himself. So much for hearing the alarm. We chatted briefly. He'd be staying to see the medal games, but most of his team had returned home. The USA flight was leaving late tomorrow. We did have a child we missed terribly and the rest of the season to play.

I'd visited with my brothers, who had flown in just for

this game, and Jared was there as well. Brady was especially hyped for a gold medal in the family lineage.

"Not that there's anything wrong with a bronze," Brady quickly said with a wobbly smile for Jared.

"It will look great next to his 2014 gold," I said proudly, and maybe a little defensively.

We'd all been super proud to see Team Canada get that bronze. Ryker had been glowing, and Jared had beamed all through their ceremony the evening before. "But no pressure," Brady had tossed out over his toast and bacon. "Just do what you do, little brother, as long as you do what you do better than anyone else," he added in that Boston accent of his. The one that he said he didn't have, but he totally did. I had rolled my eyes at my husband. Jared had simply smiled into his cup of coffee.

Jamie nudged me in the side. "But no pressure."

Laughing over the look of confusion on the eldest Rowe boy's face, I left them at the hotel, grabbed a cab to the rink, and spent an hour kicking a soccer ball around with my teammates. Coach had tried to keep it all as low pressure as possible, so no press was allowed near us once we'd entered the barn. Which was helpful. Now, oddly enough, as Tate, Colorado, and I lined up in the chute after warmups, a calm descended on me.

I'd been so torqued up about this game, Aarni, gay rights, and a thousand other things that I'd nearly stressed myself out of enjoying what might be a once-in-a-lifetime moment. Smiling at all our players as they streamed out of the dressing room, I patted each one on the backside with my stick.

Colorado tapped his blocker to every gloved hand.

Tate fist-bumped each player as he said, "Warrior Mindset" to every man who passed the captain.

Tate glanced at Colorado then me. "We ready to do this?"

"Warrior mindset," Colorado and I repeated.

Tate nodded. Colorado shoved his mask on, covered in red, white, and blue, and we followed our goalie out onto the ice for the final medal round. I wasn't a fan of afternoon games. Hockey players like their regimens, but we had no control over our schedules, be they Olympic or NHL. I would have preferred a soft morning skate and more down time before the game, personally. Still, there was a buzz in the air that infected me as the fans cheered and waved American flags. It was probably a toss-up as to which country's fanbase was louder. Sweden took hockey seriously. Every man clad in gold with blue crowns was the best of the best. Their goalie was an older player with two Stanley Cup rings to his credit. I'd always had a hell of a time scoring on him, but Tate assured me we had his number.

I wasn't sure if anyone really had Lars Fransson's number, but we'd all be doing our best to shoot high on his glove side and keep the traffic around his crease heavy. He hated a lot of men in his space, all goalies did, but Lars had a tendency to get super crabby about it. If we could lure him into lashing out with his paddle in front of a ref…

Of course, that was wishful thinking. First, we had to get to his net. The Swedes had some massive defensemen who knew us as well as we knew them. We'd all faced each other back home, so there were no surprises.

Feeling at home in my skin, I skated in for the face-off,

hunkering down to face one of the players from the western division, a sleek skater named William Holmberg.

"Good luck, loser," I tossed out as my skates settled on the hashmarks.

He chuckled. "And to you," he replied in a lovely Swedish accent.

The puck hit the ice and politeness flew out of the window. I won the face-off with ease, moving the puck to the side to Tate. And with that little win, we were off. The first period was well-played, no penalties at all, and few icings. The action was end-to-end with some quality scoring chances for both teams. Colorado and Lars were calm, settled well on their skates, and presenting themselves as huge presences in their nets.

During the first intermission Coach had little to say. "Just keep doing what you're doing offensively, but get more traffic in front of Fransson."

With that in mind, we went out for the second period, heads down, intent on getting into Lars' handsome face. Which we did, and then some. Our defenseman began getting on Lars' nerves, and by the middle of the second period, it was beginning to pay off. Nothing huge at first, but Lars was getting pushy, placing his paddle into the backs of the big D-men as his head bobbed this way and that. Our shots were still being blocked, but you could see —and hear—how pissed Lars was. He spent a good forty seconds after a shot of mine deflected off his pumpkin shouting at the refs about skaters being on his paint. Which they weren't. We were just super close. Okay, so maybe on occasion our skates *might* have drifted innocently into his space...

It was windy. Sue us.

With five minutes left on the clock, things finally opened up. I passed to Tate, who flipped the puck up and over Lars' left shoulder. That high glove-side weakness paid off with a goal. Our joy was short-lived, when Sweden—who it seemed felt that crowding the goalie was fair play for them as well as us—managed to tip one in. The deflection was slick, and Colorado never saw it sneaking under his stick arm, until the Swedes were all throwing their arms up in joy.

Tied at one goal each, we went into the second break with our game plan still locked into place. Keep shooting, keep pressuring the dynamic veteran tender, and keep forechecking.

"That's your holy trinity for the third period," Coach informed us as we rehydrated and rested.

We took the ice with determination. Colorado stood down in his crease, beating on the ice with his stick as if he were asking for the puck. He wasn't. He was just that amped-up. His energy was infectious. Tired as we were, and sore because the Swedes were forechecking just as roughly as we were, we picked up where we'd left off. Peppering the Swedish net with any kind of shot we could take. Even shitty weak ones. You just never knew when a puck might roll between the wickets or bumble along and bounce off a skate.

None of that happened at either end of the ice, but it could. Each team was playing balls to the wall. They countered each of our offensive breakaways with one of their own. Turnovers were rare. We were passing with care, keeping the puck on our sticks until we had clear lanes. Handing them the puck to open up a three-on-one would be catastrophic. The only mistake that the Swedes made was one that would eat at their head coach for months. The first penalty of the game was for too many men on the ice against Sweden. There was nothing a coach hated more than a bench penalty. Although high-sticking was one that Jared would make his men do bag skates for. He'd yell at his D-men: "Did they not teach you to keep your stick on the ice back in the peewee leagues!"

I hoped he was enjoying the game. And I hoped I would make Brady proud. As big as a pain in the ass as he was, I looked up to my brother a great deal. I prayed I could be half the player, husband, and father that he was.

Taking the power play opportunity to warp ten, we went to the net aggressively, like murder hornets or killer bees, or whatever horrid stinging insect was new on the WTF-is-wrong-with-nature news alerts. I had the pleasure of hawking Lars, putting my ass right in front of him. His blocker hit me in the lower back. I didn't move. The puck rattled around behind his net along the kickplate. I moved with the goalie, standing tall, my sight on the scrimmage in the corner. Tate was kicking at the puck to free it from under the skate of a Swedish winger.

I rocked left and right. Lars gave me a shove with his stick and called me something in Swedish I was sure wasn't a compliment. Then the puck skittered free. My first instinct was to pounce on it, but I stood my ground. Delaney Rooks, a flashy kid from Detroit, picked it up and lifted it into the air about waist-high. I twisted toward the net as Rooks fired the puck. I jerked on my stick just enough to redirect the puck upward and into the back of the net, Lars missing what would have been a beauty of a save by a mere inch.

I raced to the corner, shouting in joy, and was swallowed by my teammates. The US fans in the stands went wild.

My pulse was racing, adrenaline surging through me. I went to the bench grinning. Now all we had to do was protect that one goal lead for another seven minutes. Easy peasy. Not. So totally not. The Swedes, sensing that the momentum was now with us, came at us and Colorado with everything they had. Flurries of shots at our goalie met with either his glove, blocker, or were paddled away with a cool ease. With two-plus minutes left, Colorado came charging out of his net when one of our weary defensemen coughed up the puck. I was on the bench, gasping like a carp, when Colorado raced out between the circles and took the puck right off the stick of the incoming skater. Everyone on the bench flew to their skates and cheered the high slot robbery that had just taken place.

When the Swedes pulled their goalie with a minute-forty left, Coach barked something about grit at us as Tate and I sailed over the boards. I glanced at the time. It was going to be a long hundred seconds.

That extra attacker made his presence known. We hunkered down and threw ourselves into defensive hockey. I dove into a blistering slap shot that hit me dead center of the chest. Holy fuck, that hurt. It winded me, and I took a second or two to get to my skates. That was going to bruise. There was no time to whimper over a boo-boo though. The shots kept coming fast and furious, leaving us no time to change out, not that any of us would have anyway. I loved being on the penalty kill just for moments like this. As the clock raced down to the final seconds, I got to watch Colorado make this other-fucking-worldly scorpion kick save that would be on highlight reels for weeks. Years maybe. And then, just like that, the buzzer sounded. We mobbed Colorado, who was still spread out on the ice. We hoisted him to his skates. The bench emptied. Every man in red, white, and blue was here. We'd done it. We had fucking done it!

The next several minutes was a whirlwind of celebrating and handshakes.

"You got lucky, Rowe," Lars said.

"Madsen-Rowe. And yeah, probably so. See you in New York."

Lars gave me a nod and a pat on the shoulder, then moved on.

Things rolled along quickly, runners were thrown to the ice, some officials from the Olympic committee came out as we were lined up with the Swedes. With them were pretty Chinese women in fuzzy coats over white dresses carrying trays with gold medals. As our names were called to the crowd, a medal was handed to us, which we then draped around our sweaty necks. I thanked the man with the French accent, then the man with the Chinese accent, then the woman with the Russian accent. They all congratulated each player after giving them their medal. Our fans chanted "USA! USA! USA!" as flags billowed in the stands.

The crowd quieted when the Olympic anthem was announced in several languages. We all stood there, arms resting on the shoulders of our teammates, as the American

National Anthem began after the Olympic anthem. We sang along as a banner with the Olympic rings, our flag, the Swedish flag, and the Canadian flag climbed into the rafters. Hand resting over my heart, I wasn't sure if I had ever been prouder to be an American. Good or bad—our country had both—it was a moment steeped in national pride I'd never forget.

As much as I longed to go find my husband and brothers, there was press to contend with. *So much press*. But finally, I managed to break free from the glut of media representatives and flashbulbs. Knowing right where to find him because we might have arranged a moment for the world that had the Layton Foxx Social Media stamp of approval, Jared and I met up at a huge ice sculpture of a hockey player inside the main concourse of the rink. There was one photographer with us, a cool hipster dude with dreads named Mallory who worked for *Queer Athlete Monthly*. He was trans and a huge hockey fan. He loved all sports, but hockey was his thang. Could be because he was from Quebec. Or maybe just because hockey was the best sport in the world.

I jogged, then ran at my husband. He caught me in his arms, his smile wide, his soft blue eyes shining with admiration, love, and passion. Our lips met, pressed, and held as Mallory moved around us taking pictures. When the kiss ended, I drew back, taking Jared's face between my hands.

"Your fingers smell like rotten hockey gloves," he teased. I snort-chuckled, then kissed him once more. "I'm so proud of you. Lottie will be too."

"Lottie will use this as a teething ring." I glanced down at the gold disc resting on my chest.

"Probably, for now, but in the years to come, she'll realize what an amazing man her father is." He stared into my soul at that moment.

"You mean what amazing *men* her father*s* are."

He chuckled softly. "Yes, I did mean that. Are we done posing for polite no-tongue kisses?"

"Layton is such a buzzkill," I mock-huffed. "Yeah, meet me at the hotel room we rented. I need to shower. You think my hands stink, you should smell the rest of me."

"I can. It's not pleasant. Go shower, spend some time with your teammates, and then meet me at the hotel. Tonight, we're sharing a bed, and I plan to make love to my gold medalist husband."

Now *that* might just be better than winning gold.

Epilogue

Jared

Two Months Later

The box arrived on a Tuesday, the night after a particularly hard-won game against New York. Ten had faced Lars Fransson in a replay of the Gold Medal game, and if I was honest I'd been dreading this match-up in case there was bad blood. I needn't have worried; they were just back to being the normal kind of rivals where there were points at stake, and not gold medals.

"It's here," Tennant announced from the door to the study, Lottie with her arms curled around his neck and the large box awkwardly shoved under his other arm. I stood quickly, ready to take the box or Lottie, but it seemed as if Lottie was way more important than the parcel because he didn't let her go. I took the parcel from him and laid it gently on the huge desk Ten and I shared. His side was a clutter of hockey stuff, a pile of headshots to sign, three game pucks that needed to go on the display shelves, not to mention his share of a load of adoption and surrogacy information he and I were wading through. If I thought the challenge of having Lottie in our lives was bad enough, then adopting was a whole different ball game—or puck game, or whatever.

"Are you going to open it?" Ten asked impatiently—never one for holding back on opening anything. Last Christmas, he'd opened his presents in a record ten minutes flat, although he'd then spent the rest of the day examining them, and then kissing me each time.

I picked up the scissors and ran the blade carefully across the tape, cutting through the courier paperwork and putting that to one side. Then, I eased open the flaps and lifted out the foam packaging until we got our first look at what we'd ordered.

The case was solid wood that had been sourced from a sustainable forest, our names carved there—*Tennant and Jared Madsen-Rowe*. The glass was crystal-clear and polished, but it was what was inside that was perfect.

2014 gold and 2022 bronze medals from me, and the 2022 gold from Ten, pinned and showcased in order.

"Wow," Ten murmured, and touched the wood with reverence.

"Wow," Lottie repeated and peered into the box. I don't know how much she really understood about where her dads had been, although Ten's mom had recorded the medal ceremonies, and made this big celebration thing about what we'd won and why. It helped that when we picked her up after getting home, we'd brought chocolate medals for her to munch on, explaining that this was what we'd won.

"Choc," she said, and reached down for the glass, Ten swooping her up and away before the first of many sticky fingerprints happened. We already had the fixings up ready for the display case, and it would be way higher than a toddler could reach, but still…

"Maybe the chocolate ones were a bad idea," Ten bemoaned.

I shot him a smile. "No choc," I explained to Lottie, who blinked at me and then nodded as if she understood, and then just as quickly, reached for them again.

"Want choc!" she exclaimed.

"Not chocolate," I repeated, and her lower lip stuck out in the cutest pout I'd ever seen.

"Ooohhh, there's treats in the kitchen!" Ten exclaimed and danced our baby girl out to wherever the treats were. He came back after a short while. "She's watching *Clifford* and eating a banana," he explained, and shrugged when I huffed a laugh. Lottie was a menace with bananas, and we'd likely go out and find banana squished everywhere. Still, I needed a few moments with my husband as we settled the case up where the brackets were and tightened them as it said in the instructions.

Finally, we stood back to look at what we'd done. My cell rang with Ryker's ring tone, and I answered.

"It's here, Dad!" he said excitedly, then panned past a goat in the kitchen—I didn't ask—and to Jacob who was holding a similar case to ours, with Ryker's bronze medal. "Thank you so much."

"I love it."

"Maksim took one look at it and huffed out of the house," Ryker whispered. "But that's not stopping me putting it up right now."

"Now?" I heard Jacob say. "What about the damn goat in our kitchen?"

"Oops, gotta go, Dad, love you. Say hi to Ten."

"Hi, son," Ten deadpanned, and then the call ended—I guess the goat was an emergency.

We laced fingers and stared at the display case.

"We did good," I said, and bumped shoulders with Ten, who leaned into me and chuckled.

"Yeah, we did." He turned to face me, then pressed a soft kiss to my nose. "We probably need to go and find out where all the squished banana is."

"Good call. You go first." I encouraged him to the door with a gentle shove.

"Why me?"

"You were the one who gave Lottie the weapon of banana destruction. You need to fix it."

Tennant gave me the finger, then stole one last kiss and left to find Lottie.

"Lottie no!" I heard him say, and I couldn't help smiling. Outside of this house, we'd been rivals, but here, we were just the Madsen-Rowes—me, Ten, Lottie…

… and heaven help us, banana stuffed down the back of the sofa cushions.

Want to read how Stan handles the loss when he get's home to Erik?

Want to find out how Bryan copes with his moment with Aarni when he get's home to Gatlin?

Go here for free stories: mmhockeyromance.com/rivals-free

Hockey Series' from RJ Scott & V.L. Locey

Harrisburg Railers

Owatonna U Hockey

Arizona Raptors

Boston Rebels

LA Storm

Chesterford Coyotes - Young Adult

Free Reads

Please note - in all of these free stories, there will be some spoilers for the main series books.

Railers Short Stories

Volume 1 | Volume 2

LA Storm

Sparkle

The Colts - AHL Short Stories

Pucks & Percentages

Breakaway

Making the Save

Standalone

Waiting for Christmas

When hockey wunderkind Tennant Rowe meets his new coach, he knows he's in trouble. Jared Madsen is nine years older than Tennant, impossibly attractive, and — worst of all — his brother's off-limits best friend. Is their chemistry worth the risk?

Changing Lines (Railers 1)

Can Tennant show Jared that age is just a number, and that love is all that matters?

The Rowe Brothers are famous hockey hotshots, but as the youngest of the trio, Tennant has always had to play against his brothers' reputations. To get out of their shadows, and against their advice, he accepts a trade to the Harrisburg Railers, where he runs into Jared Madsen. Mads is an old family friend and his brother's one-time teammate. Mads is Tennant's new coach. And Mads is the sexiest thing he's ever laid eyes on.

Jared Madsen's hockey career was cut short by a fault in his heart, but coaching keeps him close to the game. When Ten is traded to the team, his carefully organized world is thrown into chaos. Nine years his junior and his best friend's brother, he knows Ten is strictly off-limits, but as soon as he sees Ten's moves, on and off the ice, he knows that his heart could get him into trouble again.

Changing Lines

Harrisburg Railers (Hockey Romance)

1. Changing Lines
2. First Season
3. Deep Edge
4. Poke Check
5. Last Defense
6. Goal Line
7. Neutral Zone
8. Hat Trick
9. Save The Date
10. Baby Makes Three
11. Rivals
12. Perfect Gifts
13. Family First

Meet the men of Owatonna University's hockey team

Ryker (Owatonna U, 1)

Ryker

Ryker is hockey royalty, Jacob is a poor country boy. Can two vastly different people find common ground and become the men they want to be?

Ryker comes from a long line of championship-winning hockey players. Playing college hockey to develop his game is his only focus, and nothing will stand in the way of him working to become the best player. He has no room for relationships, people who point out his flaws, or anyone who calls him on his dreams. He certainly has no place for love, and meeting Jacob is nothing but a useful distraction on the side. After all trying to get his Owatonna Eagles teammate into bed is less work and more play. When tragedy rocks his family, his charmed life crumbles, and the only person he can turn to is the same one who claims to hate him.

Jacob Benson has only known hard work and stifling conservative values his whole life. Born and raised in the small rural community of Eden Crossing, Minnesota, he's the only son of a hard-working but struggling dairy farming family. Jacob is using his skills in hockey to finance his way to an agricultural science degree. These four years at Owatonna U. will probably be the only time he has to enjoy life, gain acceptance about his sexuality, and live openly before his inevitable return to the farm. Running into a pretty rich boy like Ryker Madsen is putting a damper on his enjoyment of life away from home. Ryker's flip, conceited, carefree attitude grates on Jacob's every nerve. So why, if Ryker is everything he dislikes, does he want nothing more than to explore the sinful dreams that his annoying teammate stars in every night?

Ryker

Owatonna U Hockey (Hockey Romance)

Coast to Coast (Arizona Raptors 1)

Coast To Coast

When opposites attract, this bottom-of-the-league team will never be the same again.

A stipulation in his father's will forces Mark back into the arms of a family that disowned him and leaves him one-third owner of a hockey team facing financial ruin. He doesn't even watch hockey, let alone like it, and wants nothing more than to head back to New York. Then there's the new coach, a stubborn, opinionated, irritating man with superiority issues and questionable music taste. Butting heads with Rowen becomes the new normal, but it comes with passionate debate and an all-consuming lust.

Challenged to rebuild one of the worst teams in the league into a future cup contender, Rowen can't pass up the opportunity. Never in his twenty years of hockey has he ever seen a team managed so badly or coached players overflowing with resentment and bigotry. Yet there's something about this team and this city that compels him to roll up his sleeves and start dismantling. If only Mark, one of three siblings who now own the Raptors, wasn't so damned rock-headed yet so damned appealing his job might be easier. It doesn't look like either is willing to give in, but one night in a dark, desert hotel changes everything.

Coast To Coast

Arizona Raptors (Hockey Romance)

1. Coast To Coast
2. Across the Pond
3. Shadow and Light
4. Sugar and Ice
5. School and Rock

Top Shelf (Boston Rebels 1)

Acting on the attraction to his best friend's brother has always been off the table for Xander until a passionate hookup with Mason at a beach resort begins a love affair that burns long after summer ends.

Mason specializes in assisting same-sex couples on their journey to becoming parents and fighting every rule that blocks his way in the stuck-in-the-past agency that hired him. Living in his brother's pool house is rent-free, and every cent he earns he saves for his dream—that one day he'd have his own company helping others. The downside is that he has to see his annoying brother every day, the upside is that his brother's teammates from the

Boston Rebels make regular visits. The eye candy that passes Mason's window is almost enough to make him consider dating a hockey player, but not just any player though. Ever since Xander —his brother's childhood friend—came out as gay at a press conference, Mason's puppy love has turned into a burning attraction he can no longer ignore.

Hockey has been one of Xander's main focuses since he was old enough to balance on skates. Well, hockey and Mason Kingsley, but Mason was always unattainable. Now that he's about to see thirty candles on his birthday cake and is no longer hiding the fact he's gay, he's ready to find a soul mate to make his life complete. A summer vacation is just what he needs to have time to think, but when the Boston Rebels arriving in paradise with Mason in tow, thinking is the last thing he needs. One torrid night under a balmy moon and rules about not messing with his best friend's brother vanish on a warm, tropical breeze.

Summer romances don't generally last past Labor Day, but with the new season about to begin Xander and Mason are going to have to face the world and decide if their love is real enough to withstand everything.

Boston Rebels

Lost In Boston (Free Prequel Novella)

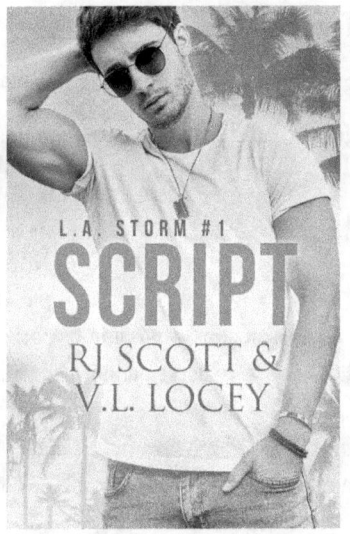

Script (LA Storm, 1)

Script

Hollywood A-lister Finn might be Canadian, but he needs Cameron to show him how to hockey.

Actor Finn Kerrigan is at a crossroads. After growing up a soap star, then starring in a hugely successful trilogy of action movies, he's finally given the chance to read a heartfelt and passionate script that could change his life forever. The role would be enough for people to see him as a serious actor, and maybe even win him an award or two (and no, a golden raspberry award for his action movies doesn't count). Once established as a serious actor he's sure he can come out of the closet and finally live his truth. When he lies to get the part of a hockey player on a struggling team, he suddenly has nowhere to hide. He might be Canadian, but the last time he skated he was ten, and no, he doesn't have hockey in his blood. With only a month until filming starts, he about to be exposed, but partnered with a player who's supposed to be giving him tips, he doesn't realize how many of his secrets will come to light. Falling in lust, one heated kiss at a time, is inevitable, but giving Cameron up at the end of the shoot could break his heart.

Cameron Chavkin is the face of the LA Storm. And the body, and the hair, and the smile. He's at the prime of his career, men and women want to be with him, and he's skating better than he ever has before. His house sits next to a famous rock star's mansion, his garage is filled with expensive cars, and he's even been asked to mentor a once-famous actor in a new hockey movie. Life is pretty sweet. Until the bad boy of hockey meets Finn, a man on the edge with more secrets than Cameron has endorsements. Knowing better than to get involved, Cameron is swept up despite himself, and when it's time to say goodbye to the Storm's most eligible bachelor is finding it hard to follow the script.

Script

LA Storm

1. Script
2. Second
3. Shield
4. Spiral

Off The Ice (Chesterford Coyotes, 1)

Off The Ice

A coming-of-age love story with high school, hockey rivalry, friendship, family, and coming out.

Soren's life changes in an instant when he and his younger brother are adopted by hockey royalty. Making sense of his new life is hard enough, but when he's enrolled in a private school it means facing a whole new set of problems. Navigating friendship, family, and hockey is one thing, but being attracted to the boy who vexes him is a whole new thing.

Felix has a reputation to protect. He's the kid who seems to have everything but looks can be deceiving. Spinning lies about his perfect life, he's created a fantasy world that even he has started to believe. Only, it's not long before everything crumbles, all of his pretty lies are revealed, and only his closest rival sees through his pain and stands by him.

Fighting is easy, friendship is hard, but love is everything.

Off The Ice

Chesterford Coyotes

1. Off The Ice
2. On Thin Ice
3. *Dance on Ice*

Also By RJ Scott

For a full list of ebooks and links please scan the code above or
visit rjscott.co.uk/rjbooks

Meet RJ Scott

RJ discovered romance in books at a very young age and realized that if there wasn't romance on the page, she could create it in her head. With over one hundred and fifty books published, she is a full time author of gay romance.

She lives and works out of her home in the beautiful English countryside, spends her spare time reading, watching films, and enjoying time with her family.

The last time she had a week's break from writing she didn't like it one little bit and has yet to meet a box of chocolates she couldn't defeat.

www.rjscott.co.uk | rj@rjscott.co.uk

NEWSLETTER - rjscott.co.uk/rjnews

facebook.com/author.rjscott

x.com/Rjscott_author

instagram.com/rjscott_author

amazon.com/author/rj-scott

bookbub.com/authors/rj-scott

goodreads.com/rjscott

pinterest.com/rjscottauthor

Also By VL Locey

For a full list of ebooks and links please scan the code above or
visit vllocey.com/stories-from-vl-locey

Meet V.L. Locey

V.L. Locey loves worn jeans, yoga, belly laughs, walking, reading and writing lusty tales, Greek mythology, the New York Rangers, comic books, and coffee.

(Not necessarily in that order.)

She shares her life with her husband, her daughter, one dog, two cats, a flock of assorted domestic fowl, and two Jersey steers.

When not writing spicy romances, she enjoys spending her day with her menagerie in the rolling hills of Pennsylvania with a cup of fresh java in hand.

vllocey.com
vicki@vllocey.com

Newsletter - vllocey.com/newsletter

facebook.com/V.L.Locey

x.com/vllocey

instagram.com/vl_locey

bookbub.com/authors/v-l-locey

goodreads.com/vllocey

pinterest.com/vllocey